URBAN

VOICE

4

New Indian Writing

First published in India 2011 by **Leadstart Publishing Pvt Ltd**
1 Level, Trade Centre
Bandra Kurla Complex
Bandra (East) Mumbai 400 051 India
Telephone: +91-22-40700804
Fax: +91-22-40700800
Email: info@leadstartcorp.com
www.leadstartcorp.com / www.frogbooks.net

Editorial Office:
Unit: 25-26 / Building A/1
Ground Floor, Near Wadala RTO
Wadala (East) Mumbai 400 037 India
Phone: +91-22-24036548 / 24036930

Sales & Marketing Office:
Unit: 122 / Building B/2
First Floor, Near Wadala RTO
Wadala (East) Mumbai 400 037 India
Phone: +91-22-24046887

US Office:
Axis Corp, 7845 E Oakbrook Circle
Madison, WI 53717 USA

Copyright © Leadstart Publishing Pvt Ltd

All rights reserved. No part of this publication may be
reproduced, stored in or introduced into a retrieval system, or
transmitted, in any form, or by any means (electronic, mechanical,
photocopying, recording or otherwise) without the prior written
permission of the publisher. Any person who does any
unauthorised act in relation to this publication may be liable to
criminal prosecution and civil claims for damages.

ISBN 978-93-81115-23-7

Typeset in Garamond
Printed at Repro India Ltd, Mumbai

Price — India: Rs 150; Elsewhere: US $10

WHY URBAN VOICE

The Indian literary scene is in the midst of a radical transformation. Indian writing in English is attracting world attention. It is no more a curiosity that once tickled the British and is accepted globally as a serious business. Foreign publishers are coming to India to set up Indian subsidies. Likewise Indian authors/publishers are exploring international rollout frameworks to establish market leadership and reputation. This has transformed not only Indian publishing, but also Indian writing as global Indians have started targeting a worldwide audience.

With the developed economies closely following the BRIC (Brazil, Russia, India, China) battle, there is renewed interest in Indian slang/phrases through emergence of web3.0 tools such as wikis, amazon, facebook, twitter, podcasts and blogs. In this truly cross-pollinated flat landscape, something mysterious and exciting is happening to Indian literature in English.

As conversations and images get increasingly captured on the 'fly', the next generation of Indian literature will evolve across diverse media platforms dissolving old hegemonies and notions. It will impact writers in other Indian languages so that even literature in Indian languages will aspire to reach global audiences as publishers vie to translate works into the German, French, Chinese, and other emerging language platforms.

URBAN VOICE, in this fourth episode, aims to capture this thrilling transformation by creating a platform for thinkers to capture 'next-in-line' trends and go beyond. This lit mag is committed to publish thought-provoking pieces from all areas in different forms.

— **Sunil K Poolani**

CONSULTING EDITORS

Ramachandra Guha
Taslima Nasreen
Sudeep Sen
Shashi Tharoor
A J Thomas
Abraham Verghese

LEADSTART PUBLISHING TEAM

Chairman & CEO: **Swarup Nanda**

Executive Director & Head, Editorial: **Sunil K Poolani**

Executive Director & Head, Editorial (Non-Fiction):
Chandralekha Maitra

Design Chief: **Mishta Roy**

Head, Marketing: **Anoo Kulkarni**

Advisor Emeritus: **Raj Supe**

Associate Editors: **Rhonda Lee Carver, Sharmila Ramnani,
Sai Prabha Kamath, Paromita Ukil, Abhirami Sriram,
Derek Bose, Shubham Gupta, Arjun Pereira**

Sales & Distribution: **Goutam Dass** *(Head, Eastern India,
Nepal, Bhutan & Bangladesh)*, **Harjeet Singh** *(Head,
Central & Western India)*, **Manohar Chapa** *(Head, South
India)*

Business Operations: **Iftikar Shaikh**

Purchase & Sales Support: **Rajesh Bale**

CONTENTS

Decline of Politics in Liberalised India

PARSA VENKATESHWAR RAO JR

ಲ

One of the promises that flickered on the horizon after the 1991 economic reforms process began was that politics is not central to the life of the nation; that the state can be pushed into the stands, and people can take charge of their own lives. There was a glimmer of this in the 1980s, too. Indira Gandhi was a different person when she came back to power for a third time in 1980 — the first two were in 1967 and in 1971 — and looked favourably on private enterprise. The old populism that fuelled her big electoral victory in 1971 was relegated to the archives as it were. Government was not all. This was further strengthened by Rajiv Gandhi, who spoke a new language of dreams and achievements. But it was the unlikely duo of prime minister P.V. Narasimha Rao and finance minister Manmohan Singh who managed to throw the old ideas out of the window and change tracks. Rao was a politician in the old mould, who was happy in manipulating and managing internecine and they did not expect the prime minister to lead the country. Rao's diminutive political stature ensured that people had at last realised that they have to fall back upon themselves. Singh was in the uninspiring mould as Rao was. It was their relative political insignificance that has made possible the marginalisation of politics.

In the troublesome 1960s and 1970s, there was not much hope for many people apart from what they could get from the many things that the state set out to do for the people, especially the poor. The few who got into the magical circle of the Indian Institutes of Technology and then on to the Indian Institutes of Management seemed to have moved away from the state and its patronage. There was, of course, the sprawling public sector, including the banks, which offered a stable job and acceptable conditions of living for the middle class. Most of us had to look for ways of getting whatever help they could get out of the government schemes. Though the state loomed ever so large in the lives of people, most of the people fended for themselves. This equation changed in the 1990s. Politicians ceased to be the masters of the country they deemed themselves to be. The real changes were happening beyond the political horizon.

It may seem paradoxical that in the decade that witnessed the decline of politics started off on a tumultuous note. It was dominated by burning political issues. First it was the reservation in government jobs — it was reckoned that there were exactly 45,000 jobs available — for other backward classes/castes based on the Mandal Commission recommendations. Prime minister V.P. Singh cunningly brought it into the public domain in 1990, in a bid to save his government and to outwit his rivals like Devi Lal. Then there was the controversy surrounding the Babri Masjid in Ayodhya, which was brought down by vandals belonging to the Vishwa Hindu Parishad, Shiv Sena, Bajrang Dal,

Rashtriya Swayamsevak Sangh, Bharatiya Janata Party (BJP), Akhil Bharatiya Vidyarthi Parishad on December 6, 1992. L.K. Advani, leader of the BJP wanted turn it into a winning card. Ironically, these two issues which were turned into the code words of Mandal and *kamandal* actually sounded the death-knell of politics. No party has been able to come to power on its own. The big and the small parties had to get into patchwork coalitions, which allowed no one to impose their agenda on the country.

Narasimha Rao seemed to have ensured through his wily functioning that no prime minister is ever taken seriously enough. There was a prelude to this diminishing stature of an Indian prime minister. V.P. Singh, Chandra Shekhar, H.D. Deve Gowda, I.K. Gujral all contributed to the fading authority of a prime minister. Atal Bihari Vajpayee was indeed on slippery ground and barely managed to restore a bit of charisma to the office. But he, too, could not sustain it because he could not assert his authority in the government and in his party. He was helpless during the 2002 post-Godhra Gujarat riots in which 2000 Muslims were massacred, and he could not take a decisive step in the wake of the 2001 terrorist attack on parliament. He wanted to be tough with Pakistan but he could not back it up with credible action. The 1998 Pokhran II nuclear explosions did not help much in elevating the status of the prime minister.

Prime ministers did not and do not matter anymore. What is emerging is collective leadership in a loose sense.

Like 1991, 2010 could prove to be a decisive turning point. The financial meltdown in the United States in 2008 triggered by the humongous housing mortgage crisis has shattered the faith in markets and brought in the global recession, which has wrecked the economies of the western world. People are unwillingly taking a second look at the state and what it could do to keep the economy on an even keel. Politicians are trying to get back into the saddle as it were, in the United States and in Europe. Politicians feel duty-bound to hector at the amoral captains of business and industry in the lawless realm of the private sector.

The signs are not yet clear in India. The young politicians are at home with their marginalised status. They are business-friendly in a sophisticated sense. Even when they address issues of poverty and backwardness, they are more likely than ever to look at the private business model of doing things with greater emphasis on efficient processes and solutions. They do not have the old ideological hang-ups even when they talk about village India and the imperatives of development.

But these young leaders look at politics through corporate lens. They feel that they must start at the bottom and move up the political leader to a position of leadership through good work. So, none of them — Rahul Gandhi, Jyotiraditya Scindia, Sandeep Dikshit, Sachin Pilot, Milind Deora, Naveen Jindal, Jitin Prasada — are in a hurry to assert themselves. They are doing their work at each of their ground zeroes in the hope that this will lay the foundation for their future ascent to the top of the power pyramid. But these are not bright leaders with innovative ideas to shape the future of the country. They are only willing to pick up off-the-shelf solutions if there are any for sale. That is, they are now looking to the experts to identify the problems and work out the solutions.

There are, of course, the middle-rung leaders like P. Chidambaram, Kapil Sibal and Jairam Ramesh who have ideas and the willingness to press forward with them. They are doing what they think needs to be done, but there visions seem to be blinkered, leaving much confusion on the trail. These three are not political in the sense it matters — of spelling out an agenda. Of connecting with the people across the country and of speaking in broader terms about how the country should move forward. Among these three, it is only Chidambaram who has been through the traditional politics but he has not managed to create an image of his own, a following of his own. But what marks out these three is that they think apolitically about issues. They do not have the basic political skills of turning a social and an economic issue into a powerful political one.

Pranab Mukherjee and A.K. Antony are the other two politicians who understand politics in the old sense of it being a continuous power game. They have the intelligence and skills to convert an issue into political ammunition. Antony did that in the Kerala assembly elections of 2004. Mukherjee displayed his political skills in the debate in parliament on the India-US civil nuclear deal in 2008.

Sonia and Rahul Gandhi depend for success on the family mystique and nothing else. The mystique is on the wane. Dynasty does not count. People have become increasingly clear-eyed and demanding. They are looking for leaders with ideas that will inspire. The mother-son duo does not have anything to offer on that front.

The man who does not understand the language of politics is prime minister Singh. He is bureaucratic in his method and narrowly programmatic in his approach. What is propping him up is the political machinery that the Congress party is.

The BJP, the main opposition party, is lacking in politicians as well. The party's leaders in parliament — Sushma Swaraj in the Lok Sabha and Arun Jaitley in Rajya Sabha — have honed their debating skills but they are not able to connect with the country at large; Swaraj is an impressive public speaker but she does not bring to her job a mind of her own and a vision of her own.

The communists are not in a happy position either. There are the politburo members like party general secretary Prakash Karat and Sitaram Yechuri, but they do not connect with the party's cadre or with the people in the country. They think hard and they have a clear political view. They do not have the ability to convert the political argument into a national agenda. The communist leaders in West Bengal like Buddhadeb Bhattacharjee and Biman Bose and in Kerala like VS Achudanandan know the political terrain of their states well. They can connect but only with the home crowd.

The media continue to focus on politics as the staple of national life but it is not so. People are not bamboozled by political rhetoric or charisma. They do listen in to the politicians and to the media but they make their own decisions. The people's decisions show that they are looking for a different kind of a politician and a different kind of politics, something that deals with their daily lives.

It is time to celebrate the death of the politician as we had known him and her till the 1970s, sounding shrill, talking big and making loud and empty promises. The present-day politician is painfully aware that the old tricks do not work. Unfortunately, they do not have anything to offer. Rahul Gandhi's feeble efforts to connect the India-U.S. civil nuclear deal with the aspirations and needs of poor people in rural India failed to impress in the debate in Lok Sabha on the issue. The fumble over Kalavati is a Freudian slip indicating a deeper uncertainty. It is not that the young Gandhi lacked the rhetoric to carry the day through but that it did not sound convincing enough. He was aware of it himself.

India has a new generation of politicians, but it does not have the new politics that will help shape the national agenda in the 21st century. The new politicians do not know what this new politics is to be.

The old issues remain. There are still too many poor people in the country. There is hunger and deprivation. People are looking for some realistic solutions to these problems. There is also an affluent class with enough ideas to chart the economic growth story that could help the poor. There is need for a politics that connects the newfound strengths to grapple with the old issues. There is need to sell new lanterns in exchange for the old ones. The present-day politicians do not know how to do this.

The decline of politics in Indian polity is good news but this is something that had happened accidentally. It is because political pygmies came on stage and people walked away. It is the small-time politicians who dealt the deathblow to politics. The man with conviction is not to be found.

The successful entrepreneur cannot hope to be the successful politician. It does not work. Business talk can never replace political debate.

ಚಿ

Social Banditry

RAMACHANDRA GUHA

ॐ

The novelist and critic, C S Lewis, said he had no time for those who thought that since they had read a book once, they had no need to read it again. The great works of literature were to read again and again. The urge to go back to a book was prompted sometimes by aesthetics, the desire to savour once more its artful or elegant prose; and, at other times, by the sense that one would learn something new on a second reading. Thus, it is said that *War and Peace* makes one kind of impression when read while young, quite another when read in middle age.

My own tastes run in the direction of non-fiction, but at least in this sphere I think I am exempt from C S Lewis's strictures. Among the books I go back to are autobiographies, such as those written by Neville Cardus, G H Hardy, Mahatma Gandhi, Verrier Elwin, Salim Ali and Leonard Woolf. I have also read Tagore's tract on nationalism three or four times, and C L R James's *Beyond a Boundary* at least once every other year.

These return journeys have chiefly been undertaken for pleasure. However, I recently reread a book for instruction.

Like some other Indians, I have been thinking a great deal recently about the rise of the Maoist movement in the country. Who or what are these Maoists? Are they, as the home ministry tells us, a bunch of thugs and murderers, or are they, as some left-wing intellectuals claim, idealistic and high-minded revolutionaries who shall create a society free of evil and exploitation?

In search of answers, I went back to a book I had first read 25 years ago. In the 1980s, while writing a doctoral thesis on peasant resistance in the Uttarakhand Himalaya, I had read the works of British social historians who had written about lower-class protest in early modern England. Within that vast and once very influential literature, I thought that one study in particular might help clarify my ideas about the Maoists now active in central and in eastern India. This was E J Hobsbawm's book, *Bandits*.

And so I read that book again. I learnt (or learnt afresh) that there is an important distinction to be made between the ordinary criminal and what Hobsbawm calls the "social bandit". Whereas the former is despised by poor and rich equally, the latter "never cease[s] to be part of society in the eyes of the peasants (whatever the authorities say)". "The point about social bandits," writes Hobsbawm, "is that they are peasant outlaws whom the lord and state regard as criminals, but who remain within peasant society, and are considered by their people as champions, avengers, fighters for justice, perhaps even leaders for liberation, and in any case as men to be admired, helped and supported."

Hobsbawm was writing about another continent and another century. Still, his book does seem to speak somewhat to the India of the present. In an evocative passage, he writes of social bandits in medieval Europe that "they lived their wild, free lives in the forest, the mountain caves, or on the wide steppes, armed with the 'rifle as tall as the man', the pair of pistols at the belt?, their tunics laced, gilded and crisscrossed by bandoleers, their moustaches bristling, conscious that fame was their reward among enemies and friends."

This description, with a word or phrase changed or modified, could fit the current *bete noire* of the West Bengal state government, the Maoist leader who uses the *nom de plume*, Kishenji. To be sure, he wears a cloth mask rather than a moustache, while, to broadcast his fame (and notoriety), he uses those very modern devices, the cellphone and the television camera. However, the way he speaks and the manner he affects bring to mind the swagger and self-regard of the medieval social bandit. Like that character, Kishenji will be wild, and he will be free — and he thinks the police will never catch him.

Hobsbawm observes that in several countries and historical epochs (as for example, early-20th-century Mexico), bandits had joined revolutionary political struggles, "not because they understood the complexities of democratic, socialist or even anarchist theory, but because the cause of the people and the poor was self-evidently just, and the revolutionaries demonstrated their trustworthiness by unselfishness, self-sacrifice and devotion — in other words by their personal behaviour". Then, he continues, "That is why military service and jail, the places where bandits and modern revolutionaries are most likely to meet in conditions of equality and mutual trust, have seen many political conversions."

Once more, the parallels with the current crop of Naxalites are not hard to detect. What they have going for them is their lifestyle — they can live with, and more crucially, live like the poor peasant and tribal, eating the same food, wearing the same clothes, eschewing the comforts and seductions of the city. In this readiness to identify with the oppressed, they are in contrast to the bureaucrat, the politician and the police officer. And to take Hobsbawm's other point, from the late 1960s onwards, the jail has indeed been a crucial site for the transmission of Maoist ideology in India.

Historical comparisons are never exact. In some respects, the Indian Maoists are like the social bandits of early modern Europe. They too emerged in response to inequalities in society and the manifest corruptions of the State. With the government indifferent to the needs of the poor, a band of motivated individuals have come forward to identify with their interests.

Here, the parallels break down. For the Maoists seek not justice for a single individual or village, but a wholesale reordering of society. Their ambitions are far larger than, for example, those of the late Koose Muniswamy Veerappan, he of the bristling (and outsize) moustache. Whereas the gang of that Tamil Robin Hood operated in a single hill range, the Maoists have a network stretching across several states.

Hobsbawm wrote of the bandits he studied that "they are not activists and not ideologists or prophets from whom novel visions or plans of social and political organisation are to be expected". The Maoists, on the other hand, see themselves as ideologists and even prophets, although it must be said that their vision and plan are not novel but wholly derivative. They hope that, in time, they will prevail by the force of arms over the Indian State, thus to capture power in New Delhi much as their revered hero, Mao Zedong, had captured power in Beijing 60 years ago.

This larger aim marks them out from the likes of Veerappan, as, of course, does their access to more deadly weapons such as AK-47s, dynamite and landmines, not to speak of their practice of a virtual cult of violence which takes pleasure in blasting transmission lines and railway stations and beheading policemen and alleged informers. As it happens, however, the revolutionary dreams of the

Maoists are a fantasy. The Indian State is far more powerful today than the Chinese State was back in the 1940s. And in spite of all its manifest faults and failures, most Indians prefer our current, multiparty democracy to a one-party state to be run by the Maoists.

For these, and other, reasons, we must withhold from them their own preferred appellation, that of "revolutionaries". They are considerably less than that, but also far more than ordinary criminals. Should we then see them as social bandits for a postmodern age, capable, like their medieval counterparts, of irritating the hell out of the government of the day, if ultimately incapable of overcoming or replacing it?

৪০

So Betrayed

SHASHI WARRIER

౭ಾ

A few years ago, travelling through Chhattisgarh, I stopped for the night at a small hotel in Bhilai. I needed to photocopy some papers, and, after dark, I set out to find a shop with a copier. A few hundred metres from the hotel was a shop that advertised XEROX in black letters on a yellow board outside. A wiry young man stood behind the counter, and I stepped in to hand him the papers. As I did so, however, the power failed.

As the man behind the counter lit a candle, I saw that this wasn't just a photocopy shop: there were three computers behind: an internet café. One other customer waited. The youngster took the papers and offered me a seat, telling me that the power would soon be restored, and I sat down to wait. He served the other customer, then held out an open packet of biscuits. I helped myself, and sat down to chat.

It turned out that the young man, Mukesh, was from Bhopal. He'd been three years old that winter's night when the gas leaked out Union Carbide's plant. His immediate family – father, mother, two siblings, and, of course, himself

– had been out visiting relatives in Indore and had returned to scenes of benumbing loss and devastation. Of entire neighbourhoods of dead and dying.

He tried to tell me of the enormity of the event. "In those days," he explained, "Bhopal was not a big city. There were maybe ten lakh people there, I don't know exactly, but it must be about that. I don't know how many died, but I know that thousands did. All the hospitals were full, and there was mourning everywhere. I think one in three people in our *mohalla* died, because the wind blew the gas towards us. I can't imagine how many people were affected: everyone was, to some extent. Some got over it in the next few days, but many never did. The whole city went sick: we knew that life would never be the same again."

We chatted without disturbance. People went by outside, but no one came in. In the light of the candle there was the illusion of closeness, and Mukesh knew I would leave town next morning, that my base was half a country away: I could do him no harm, so he could speak to me safely. And speak he did, without bitterness or rancour, but with a maturity I thought rare in a man so young.

Among the victims were Mukesh's relatives. His father's uncle, staying in the next street, had also been away at work outside town, and had returned to find his wife and daughters seriously ill.

Over the next few weeks, this man had lost everyone but one granddaughter, Sonu, then an infant. Now, over sixty, a pensioner, he and his granddaughter lived with Mukesh.

The granddaughter would have been in her early twenties, I calculated. "Does she go to college?" I asked.

"No," came the reply. "She can't."

"Why not?"

"She's not well. She has these terrible headaches, and asthma. She's very weak. She has some... some mental problems, besides. But she can read and write… not much, just a little."

"All this from the gas?"

"Yes."

"But didn't they get any help?"

"*Sahib*, what help? The government thought only of two kinds of help: money and medicines. *Bade chacha* [that's what he called his father's uncle] himself was unwell. Who was there to run after the doctors to get a medical certificate and then after the clerks to get some money?"

"So he got nothing?"

"He got the certificates, finally. He paid everyone, got certificates saying that his wife and children died from the gas, and finally he got Rs 25,000. He got medical certificates saying that he and Sonu are sick because of the gas, and when he went to the hospital the clerk wanted money to let them see the doctor. He paid, and saw the doctor, and then he had to pay the x-ray man because the doctor ordered a chest x-ray for the child.

"It wasn't worth it. He had to travel in a bus for an hour to get to the hospital, wait there for two or three hours to see the doctor, pay the clerk… Each time he wanted to see the doctor he lost a whole day, and had to pay for that. He went to a private doctor near his house. This doctor used to give him some medicines free, and he took only half the fee, he didn't make them wait more than fifteen or twenty minutes, and he didn't order any unnecessary tests, so it was cheaper.

"That private doctor, he was much better than the government fellows. Of course, he also took money, but at least he took only half his usual fee, and he gave whatever medicines he could, samples. He used to ask medical reps for more samples of whatever he could give people here. Even the medical reps used to distribute more free samples here. As much as they could."

"Why did you leave, then?"

"We had to leave, for the same reason so many people left Bhopal. The water was bad. Everyone was sick. So many people had died. My father had relatives in Raipur – that was part of Madhya Pradesh then. So he got a job there, and we shifted.

"Were things better there?"

"After a year or two, it seemed much the same. We had a smaller house, but otherwise we were okay. I was very small then, and didn't know much. But afterwards Papa told me that his salary was lower in the beginning. It took a few years for him to settle down properly. After that it was all right. He's still there, with my mother and my sisters."

"How did you happen to come here from Raipur?"

"I have another uncle here, my father's younger brother, who has a good job with the steel plant. He lives alone: he never got married. A few years ago, about the time Chhattisgarh was formed, he asked me if I would like to shift here to look for a job, because the place was growing very fast. And *Bade chacha* wanted to come here, away from Raipur and Bhopal."

"Why was that?"

"That doctor in Bhopal was good. He told us that the girl had mental problems that could be treated. He told us something about PTSD but how could we take her to a psychiatrist right there? Who will marry her if they know she's been treated for mental illness?

"So *Bade chacha* came here with me so that she could see a psychiatrist. We didn't want to do that in Raipur or Bhopal, close to our relatives. Now, if the treatment works, if she gets better, then he can think of going back and finding her a husband. We'll think of something to tell them to explain her absence all this while."

"Is she better now?"

He shakes his head. "I don't know. We all hope she'll improve, but the treatment started so many years after the tragedy… Fifteen, sixteen years after. Maybe it was too late. Now she goes to a psychiatrist, she takes her medicines, she goes to a counselor, but there's not much improvement. Of course, the psychiatrist says we should never give up."

"And what does *Bade chacha* think?"

"What can he do? He only thinks of her future. His big worry is this: who will take care of her when he is gone? If he loses hope that she will get better, he will break down."

"How long will he try?"

"As long as he can. He is also unwell, you see, but he can manage for himself. He had a job that gives him a small pension. He's been trying to fix it so that Sonu gets it after he dies, but that's not possible… But his employers gave him something. I don't remember how much, but they tried.

"See, everyone on the street helped. That kept us going. Even during the worst, there were people helping each other. That was the mood. You didn't ask questions. You did what you could… But I did notice one strange thing."

"What?"

"I didn't notice it: *Bade chacha* did. Even though the gas spread all over, no one in the richer areas, like Arera Colony, was affected. The gas didn't go anywhere near a leader's house. Isn't that strange?"

Come to think of it, yes, it was strange. Perhaps the better off lived in houses in salubrious green areas further away from the factories and the pollution. I kept quiet, and he continued, "*Bade chacha* used to keep saying this: maybe if some politician's children had been affected, matters would have been different."

I was based in Coimbatore at the time, and I remembered that the death of the son of a local politician had provoked the city government into building a pedestrian bridge across a major road at a busy crossing. Many others had died there, with no response from the government.

"You said he used to keep saying it," I said. "What does he say now?"

He blinked, and looked down for a moment. "*Sahib*, he is not a bad man. You must understand this. He has never broken a law, except to bribe those people at the hospital. But he says that he wishes that some of Arjun Singh's children had died… he prays that if anything like this happens in future, some big people must lose what we have lost…"

I didn't know what to say to that, so we sat in silence. By and by the power came back, and I got my copies. Before leaving, I asked him if I could email him. He gave me his email ID, and I used one of his computers to send him an email. "Keep in touch," I told him as I left.

We did keep in touch after that. By and by we exchanged telephone numbers, and I spoke to *Bade chacha* as well. When I spoke to them after the Bhopal judgment, I was grateful that the people of that city aren't violent: they have suffered enough provocation for a hundred Maoist-type movements.

So here is an update. Mukesh is married, and his shop is doing well. *Bade chacha* is in his seventies, healthy for his age, and takes care of Sonu, who is a little better. She works part-time, but is still on medication, and her headaches, asthma, and depression persist. She is not married, and her grandfather has little hope of finding her a husband.

A few days after the judgment came more news, even more shameful: the group of ministers asked to look into the matter of compensation for victims came up with a figure of Rs 1,500 crore worth. Mukesh doesn't understand this. He told me that the government, back in the 1980s, had asked Union Carbide for $3 billion before settling out of court for $470 million. Given that we know that the damage is much greater than we knew at that time, and accounting for inflation, any estimate of compensation must be at a few times the $3 billion demanded then. In other words, the compensation must be of the order of $5 billion or more, a minimum of Rs 23,000 crore. This estimate is just insult added to injury, and it's made matters stunningly clear: the Indian government will not stand by any of the country's poor or ill-connected citizens. Keshub Mahindra gets more sympathy from the government than the families of the 15,000 (or is it 20,000?) dead.

To those of us who criticize George W Bush for his sanguinary invasions, here is a sobering thought: Bush killed foreigners. Our government kills its own. I am ashamed to be an Indian.

The last time I spoke to *Bade chacha*, he told me once again that he prays thus: if a disaster ever strikes again, a minister's child's should die, for that might bring relief to common folk. Nothing else will.

Prayer Flag

SUDEEP SEN

ॐ

1. MANAS SAROVAR, MT. KAILASH

Frayed, flapping in the high winds —
   prayer flags gently unravel —
homage to the day's first light.

But today, the dawn is not as bright,
   though heavy, brooding, silver-grey
like the lake's shimmering glass-top.

No one is here, except for a woman
   staring far away,
wrapped in her sanctity

of continuous linen — her own sari
   like a prayer flag —
though devoid of any colour.

She isn't mourning or crying,

just gazing fixedly
into the water's changing glimmer,

as the sky's wet weight
   and the shore's rocky line meet,
their edges meanderingly

melting into the lake itself.
   I stood far behind her,
behind everything she saw.

2. PRAYER FLAGS

She was only
   an accidental figure
in the wide-screen frame.

Unlike her,
   I was looking skywards,
through the prayer flag's

translucent cotton,
   counting each thread
of each piece of cloth

that wove private stories,
   whispered *only* to me.
Weather-worn, strung across

canted multiple horizons,
   I tried to map
their own geographies —

each an island,

each with its own terrain, texture,
inscription, and scripture.

Found on the highest points
    on land, as close to the sky
as is possible,

these magic carpets —
    shapes caught on
an unintentional clothes-line —

were more meaningful to me
    than this vast
monastic scenery.

How each flag — each one,
    must have preserved secrets
that *only* their owners knew.

How each, a talisman —
    exuded safety and calm —
shrouding away grief

for the briefest while,
    when one forgets everything —
real, imagined — and just dreams.

3. PILGRIMAGE

My own piece of cloth
    that I'd once tied onto this line,
wasn't visible to me now.

But that did not matter.

I found strength in this
procession of private passion,

in these flags' lack of starch
   or hierarchy.
Their stories passed down

by one flag to another,
   toggled hand in hand
through time and age —

just like my pet yellow butterfly
   who infused each flower
in my garden with the gift of life

without any show or fare. I like
   the transparent quiet here — I also
like the wind's occasional sound,

its severe current tearing through
   the flag's heart—picking out
the perfect pitch and melody.

4. Buddha in a Lotus

A memory now, a still — framed,
   not revealing to the world
what I had once seen —

the panorama's generosity,
   its wild, stark untouchability.
How each story

stitched and preserved

like the jewel in the lotus —
its crystal-fine edges

caressed by petal's soft skin —
until,
everything folds inward —

like a foetus in a womb,
a toppled misplaced comma,
my own implanted memory.

And then, they bloom,
fanning outward —
each flag, strand, story,

each private grief and pleasure —
chanting noiselessly
in the mountain's silent winds.

*[Inspired, in part, by 'Pilgrim and Prayer Flags at Manas':
a photograph by Deb Mukharji]*

৪৩

A Goddess, a Snake and a Double-Edged Sword

MARGARET MASCARENHAS

ఈ

On June 6, 2004, drivers on the Avenida Francisco Farjardo in the city of Caracas, capital of Venezuela, witnessed a bizarre sight: the landmark statue of Maria Lionza, commissioned by the 50s' regime of Perez Jimenez from sculptor Alejandro Colina, had cracked in two. The torso of the goddess had fallen backwards, leaving her staring helplessly at the heavens. Oddly enough, according to news reports, this occurred a day after authorities announced the completion of restoration treatment. The imposing monument of reinforced concrete, which normally stands 11.2 metres high, had not been moved for the restoration process, and was surrounded by scaffolding at the time of the collapse, creating a bizarre cage-like visual effect. According to a BBC news story, "When Venezuelans awoke on 6 June to find Maria Lionza broken at the waist, interpretations and conspiracy theories abounded. Some said the goddess had broken in two deliberately in order to warn Venezuelans about the danger of their deeply-divided nation." (BBC, *The Goddess and the President*, June 21, 2004.)

Having grown up in Venezuela, for me, this story became the irresistible seed material for a novel, titled *The Disappearance of Irene dos Santos*, which was picked up by Hachette USA. A novel by a Goan about Venezuela? As it happens, that is where I grew up. And I don't subscribe to the prevailing belief among mainstream publishers in India that novelists of Indian origin need restrict themselves to content on India, Indian subjects, Indian characters. This is an ostrich-like mentality that profoundly weakens the published literary output of Indian writers, and is driving them increasingly to alternative publishing. Moreover, it hardly makes sense, with Venezuela's President, Hugo Chavez, attracting worldwide attention as an even bigger Bad Boy than Castro in the eyes of the US government, it seems opportune to present Venezuela, and its contemporary political history, from a different perspective. So I, a novelist of Indian origin, am going to tell you a little about the Venezuela I know. Specifically, I am going to tell you about Maria Lionza, a political symbol for the Venezuelan masses, and the power of storytelling as a catalyst for change.

Maria Lionza, a 16th century tribal Indian princess/goddess, is a cultural archetype much like many Indian deities, that has captured the imagination of the Venezuelan population. The number of people who believe in her number in the hundreds of thousands. Given strong impetus in the 1950s by dictator Marcos Perez Jimenez, who made Maria Lionza a symbol of national identity, the cult has been officially recognised and sanctioned by subsequent democratic governments of Venezuela even though the existence of Maria Lionza herself has yet to be authenticated by scholars of the period, and she is still considered to be the patron saint of the nation. The mythical origins, of Maria Lionza, handed down by oral tradition, are lost in time. The version I have given in the novel is an amalgamation of four of the most popular stories of her origin.

Though believed to have many incarnations, the goddess is generally depicted in two forms: (1) as Yara, naked, riding a tapir, and holding a human pelvis in her upstretched arms; (2) as Maria, a mestiza Virgin-Mary figure wearing a blue mantle over her head and shoulders. Maria Lionza reigns over her subjects from the Sorte Mountain in the state of Yaracuy along with a pantheon of deities that includes real and legendary characters from Venezuelan history. Officially known as the Maria Lionza National Park, Sorte is frequented by large numbers of pilgrims and tourists, particularly on weekends and holidays.

The primary deities in the goddess's pantheon, which is divided into "courts, include 'el Libertador', Simon Bolivar, the man who fought for and won the independence of many Latin American countries, 'el Negro Felipe', a black man who is said to have fought with Bolivar in the Independence Wars; 'el Indio Guaicaipuro', who is believed to have fought against the Conquerors at the time of the Conquest. But there are numerous other sub-deities such as writer Andres Bello, and even a common criminal known as El Malandro Ismael, whose veneration is outside the realm of traditional perceptions of 'goodness' and 'morality'.

When Maria Lionza is in her 'Virgin-Mary' form, el Negro Felipe, and el Indio Guaicaipuro also appear. Together, they are called 'Las Tres Potencias' (the Three Powers), representing the three races that make up the Venezuelan population.

In her tribal avatar, Maria Lionza is the reverse of the most frequently represented image of Simon Bolivar: she rides the gentle tapir, he rides a stallion; she is nude, he wears an army uniform; she holds a symbol of life (a human pelvis), he holds a symbol of death (a sword).

Catholicism is the predominant religion of Venezuela

and a majority of Marialionceros are Catholic. Although the Catholic Church frowns upon the worship of the pagan goddess, it has abandoned efforts to eradicate it. Maria Lionza's devotees come from all races and classes, but she is especially revered among the poor.

To my knowledge, no Venezuelan radio- or tele-novella, has been written specifically about Maria Lionza or her incarnations to date, which is quite extraordinary, given that she is the emblem of all the hopes and aspirations of Venezuela's masses. I myself have used the myth primarily as signifier and anchor in *The Disappearance of Irene dos Santos*.

Kidnappings, forced disappearances, and assassinations orchestrated by revolutionaries, crime bosses, the secret police, or international mercenaries have long been a part of the Venezuelan story. In 1976, when I was in high school, the father of a former schoolmate, William Niehaus, an American businessman, was kidnapped by the Grupo de Comando Revolucionario, guerilla wing of the Liga Socialista, and held for over three years. Around the same time charismatic media personality, Renny Ottolina, beloved by the masses, was killed after deciding to run for President as an independent, just three months before elections. The crackdown on the drug trade in Colombia has forced much of it across the border, and these days Venezuela is a very dangerous place to travel. The nexus between drug-running and gun-purchase by groups such as FARC continues. And largely, this story remains untold.

The roots of the popular Latin-American novella, extend back to the days of the Cuban "radio lectores", readers hired to read social realist novels of the 19th century to workers in cigar factories. With the advent of radio was born a genre of melodrama that depicted social ills in a more popular and less literary format. It was called the "culebrón" (snake) because of its tendency to go on extending itself as long as the audience for it existed, and it was the precursor of the tele-novella. Not surprisingly, the tele-novella's global export came via Cuban exiles at the end of the 50s and early 60s, many of whose writers and directors fled to Venezuela, Argentina and Mexico.

It was in Mexico that a new form of serialized storytelling emerged pioneered and developed by Miguel Sabido for Televisa where he was vice-president for research in the 70s. The essence of the Sabido Method was the use of the soap opera to educate and encourage social change. It was a new communication model that has had enormous global impact. Using the classic literary device of character growth, Sabido developed the process of character transformation in a way that was television-specific and tackled sensitive subjects such as sex, abortion, family planning, and AIDS in an accessible manner. It is a method that has been adopted and adapted all over the world. Obviously, such a mechanism for influencing the masses can be a double-edged sword...

Venezuela, one of the world's major oil-exporting nations which also boasts a vast rainforest, has one of the most vibrant cultures I know of. The country is currently engaged in a fascinating political experiment, and on this subject, it is a country deeply divided. I have met some who are passionately for it, and others who are vehemently against it. I have no idea how it will turn out, but it promises to be a wild ride. Perhaps we in India might learn something from it.

ॐ

The Sea, the Sea

KALPISH RATNA

ಠಿ

Six years ago, visiting a friend on Willingdon Island, I woke to find myself on Mars. I was in the backwaters of the Periyar river on a pisciculture farm. To get here I had passed a quaint mosque at Kodungalloor built by Cheraman Perumal in 628 C.E. A plaque identified it as 'India's First Masjid'. What I loved was its tranquil marriage of Hinduism and Islam.

I was told Muchiripattinam had been a prosperous port near here in days of old. *Muchiri* is Malayalam for cleft lip and describes the three tributaries of the Periyar that open into the Arabian Sea. Kodungalloor is the Muchiripattinam of yore, the Muziris* of the *Periplus*.

It was dawn and an eerie silence engulfed the farm. The air held its breath. The sea was a streak of light scoring the tautened sky. Sand shuffled underfoot, disowning moisture. I left the beach and walked towards the village. Here too, no life stirred. My approach did not send hens

---

* Recent excavations have located Muziris at Pattinam not Kodungalloor.

skittering across the path. Two stray dogs stood about morosely sniffing the horizon. The silence was so complete that I grew aware of my heartbeat.

I went indoors. My friend laughed at my baffled expression.

'Go back out at ten,' he advised.

I did so five minutes short of the hour.

The air had altered. A frisson of expectation ruffled the trees. Birds looked up, fanning out their wings. The hens were out now. They trooped sedate and decorous behind the rooster who strolled like some rakish boulevardier, beak skyward, testing the air. The dogs were waiting. They followed me to the beach and circled me edgily, catching my eye with an intelligence I couldn't read. They growled throatily and sprang away with glad barks, racing madly up and down the beach. They had seen it first.

The birds took off.

The sand bristled between my toes.

Then the air cracked wide, the sun slid out, and the sea came in.

Everything moved — trees, birds, insects, children. Even those hens skidded in a brainless scuttle. The land, flat-lined since dawn, was vivified now, growing a thready rhythm of life, as it picked up its vital signs from the sea.

> *Of shoes and ships and sealing wax,*
> *Of cabbages and kings*
> *And why the sea is boiling hot*
> *And whether pigs have wings.**

*** The Walrus and the Carpenter** by **Lewis Carroll**. From *Through the Looking-Glass and What Alice Found There; 1872.*

Ships

Ghodbunder is a dusty little village with a fort on a hill at the end of a crumbling dirt road. The domed castle once housed the Portuguese Viceroy Martim Affonso Sousa. Ghodbunder was then a strategic port through which the Portuguese controlled the trade in Arabian horses.

Shivaji was beaten here in 1672. The fort was finally captured by the Marathas in 1737. There's a school here now, and I walked past a scrimmage on the old battlefield.

I hadn't come to Ghodbunder seeking heroes and horses. I had followed the purring back of the creek, gleaming now before me, curved like a cat in the sun.

Bassein Creek is one of the few inland seas left in Bombay. To the north lie Vasai, Agashi, and Sopara, historical ports all.

Sopara — Surparaka of old — is mentioned in the inscriptions at Kanheri, and by every European chronicle of that time. Agashi was important in the 13th and 14th centuries, and Vasai was the Portuguese stronghold in the 16th.

I stood between two estuaries, Vaitarna to my north and Ulhas east of me. All the way to Thana from here are ports that have ebbed in importance and fortune as they have changed location.

In Arab maps of the 15th century, Vasai and Agashi-Sopara are separate islands. The Portuguese port of Vasai was situated on the west of Panju Island. The channel between the Ulhas estuary and Panju Island is now constricted, and allows only small craft. This constriction, and the subsequent choking of the creek happened after railway tracks were laid on these embankments.

The Portuguese shipyard was in the north of Vasai Island. Between Vasai and the village of Gus-Nirmal on Agashi–Sopara are tidal flats. In the past, the two islands were separated by a body of water. Satellite imagery shows the ancient boundaries of Vasai and Agashi as separate islands.

As I watched, a dhow with a brightly painted prow sailed serenely past. Portuguese ships built in the Vasai and Papdi yards were huge (1,000 tons or more) by the standards of that time. Wouldn't they have demanded wider draft than what nature afforded?

No, according to today's mariners.

Rice was exported from Bhatibunder, the old port at Agashi. Coastal craft probably transported cargo to the larger ships anchored out at sea. The need to artificially widen these ports probably never arose in the 16th century. This would happen elsewhere along the coast, in the next century, soon after the British took over Bombay.

A hundred years later, the scene appears strongly reminiscent of that time.

The shore is banked with black pyramids of silt and damp sand. The strand bustles with lorries and handcarts that fill up and move away at an astonishing rate. This is the sand mafia at work, poaching illegally on the coastline.

But there was nothing clandestine about such activity in Bombay's past. Water channels were dredged to accommodate larger craft. Though the term, I'm told, applies only to the massive operations necessitated by steam shipping, the de-silting and widening of waterways is surely as old as sailing itself.

From my vantage atop the hill, this sand extraction has taken a considerable bite out of the coast. A large crescent at the water's edge has been dug up. The muddy swirl of grey reaches far out into the water. As spoilage piled up, embankments would slowly erode, and crumble into the water.

The ports of north Bombay have migrated downstream over the centuries, mainly because creeks and tidal inlets have been choked by the debris of this overbuilt city as roads and railways carve space for themselves.

Shoes

The summit of Ghodbunder fort is a revelation. I look down through a series of arches in infinite regression until Martim Affonso's vulgar palace blocks the horizon. If I climb over the broken stones that once made up a rampart, I can see past that white cupola and follow the wide arc of the creek. Closer, is the built up side of the hill. A straggle of tin-roofed shacks is all that remains of this port city. In the west, tidal flats have been reclaimed as far as eye can see, and bald patches of land occasionally gleam between the pink-and-brown scruff of buildings that peel with industrial eczema. Pylons rear up from the marsh like bare masts of ghost ships — carracks, East Indiamen — as if we need reminding that they stand rooted in the sea.

Islands are marine organisms that breathe from tidal flushes of water. So what happened to this one over 500 years?

Its gills are no more.

Streams, creeks and tidal inlets have been erased; rivers are buried under layers of human detritus; the land is porous no longer, its drainage is choked off.

Over time the islands of Bombay have become an extension of the mainland. Like a cancer, the city has cancelled its own geography, seeped its toxins into its surrounds, decayed and fragmented its foundations by leaching out nutrients that imbue life.

Before European contact, Bombay lived by trade and agriculture. The port received merchandise that ships carried across the sea. Besides silk and brocade from the factories of Thana, trade chiefly was in perishable foods — rice, fruit, vegetables, and fish. Luxuries weren't lacking, but life on the islands was hard work and sufficiency.

Then came the Portuguese. Life became a succession of traumatic interruptions and, after 1510, there loomed also the specter of displacement. Lightning attacks by Portuguese 'heroes' like Heitor da Silveira were really slave raids. People were captured, taken to Goa, and put to work building churches. Then in

1534 when João de Castro apportioned lands, the farmers that still remained could till their own land as slaves. Simon Botelho recorded on 10 October 1554:

Some of these villages were abandoned, others lapsed by death, some were granted to new persons and others were rented. Thus no credit can be given to the names of persons to whom these villages were granted in 1548.

A perusal of Portuguese revenues shows a steady annual increase from 1540, clearly from the agricultural land they appropriated. More and more land was brought under cultivation. The rice grown in Shashti fed Portuguese Goa. The foothills of the Sahyadris were cleared to increase arable land, and the swamps and marshes were drained. Simon Botelho offered advise in 1560 that 'drowned lands' should be filled to provide better revenue. The 'wash' between Worli and Mazagaon was partly filled during this period, enough to provide *kharabhat*, a wild rice that grew in the salt pans and tidal areas.

The ground between this and the great breach is well ploughed and bears good batty. '(Fryer, 1695)

At low tide, the islands of 17th century Bombay offered a view of what they would grow into. Antonio de Mello Castro protested to the Portuguese King in a letter dated 5 January 1666, shortly after the British takeover:

The first act of Mr. Humphrey (Cooke), who is the Governor of the Island, and whom I knew in Lisbon as a grocer, was to take possession of the island of Mahim in spite of my protests, the island being some distance from Bombay… He argues that at low tide one can walk from one to the other, and if this is conceded your

Majesty will be unable to defend the right to the other northern islands as at low tide it is possible to go from Bombay to Salsette, from Salsette to Varagaon *

The original seven islands of Bombaim did not include Salsette. They were Kola-Bhat, Al-Omani, Bombaim (Girgaum), Macchagaon, Varli, Parell-Sewri, and Newala or Baradbat (Mahim).

Portuguese interests were centred in Salsette. They didn't much care for the southern territories and these were the islands they ceded to the British. These new owners identified the swamps between Bombaim and Mazagaon and the 'great breach' as insalubrious. Then came Gerald Aungier's grand plan for Bombay and the influx of a large work force. The seven islands were welded by the end of the 17th century into Bombay-Mazagaon, Colaba-Al-Omani, and Parel-Worli-Mahim.

More breaches were filled — between Mahim, Dharavi and Sion, Mahim and Worli, Worli and Cumballa Hill. In a city steadily robbed of its natural drainage this translated into a constant eruption of 'fluxes' — diarrheas and dysenteries.

Fryer and Ovington and chroniclers of The East India Company relate mainly European woes. Liver complaints were linked to the English attraction to 'fool's rack.'**Amebic hepatitis is a more probable diagnosis.

Reclamation removes an island's first defence against

---

* *Tratados* Vol III, page 94; *The Portuguese in India* Volume II, pages 355-357; quoted in Gerson da Cunha's *The Origin of Bombay*; page 265

** **Fool's rack:** The actual Urdu is *phool ka arq,* 'a distillation from a flower.' *Arq* is also any strong drink or 'distilled spirit.' *Phool* is 'flower.' Fool's rack refers to *toddy,* a distillate of the date palm, *arq al-tamar.* Hence the corruption *Fool's rack.* The Europeans added sea blubber to make it even more disease — its mangroves. Mangroves trap effluents and prevent the eutrophication of coastal waters as they degrade organic matter and recycle it as food for coastal fauna. Without them, effluents issue unchecked, and uncleansed, into the sea.

Our awareness of the importance of mangroves is very recent. The British were particularly energetic about clearing swamps.

The final decades of the 18th century were marked by dockyards as Bombay's shipbuilders assured her maritime glory. The Hornby Vellard*** was completed in 1838 and united all seven islands of Bombay. It sealed off 'the Great

---

abominable. Here are Garcia and Fryer writing of the same thing a hundred years apart:

'... this çura they distil like brandy (*agna ardente*): and the result is a liquor like brandy; and a rag steeped in this will burn as in the case of brandy; and this fine spirit they call *fula*, which means 'flower'; and the other quality that remains they call *orraca*, mixing with it a small quantity of the first kind. ...'

—Garcia da Orta ; 1563.

'Among the worst of these (causes of disease) Fool Rack (Brandy made of *Blubber*, or *Carvil*, by the Portugals, because it swims always in a Blubber, as if nothing else were in it; but touch it, and it stings like nettles; the latter, because sailing on the Waves it bears up like a *Portuguese Carcil*. It is, being taken, a Gelly, and distilled causes those that take it to be Fools. ...'

—Fryer; 1673.

Hobson-Jobson—*A Glossary of Colloquial Anglo-Indian Words and Phrases* by **Henry Yule, Arthur Coke Burnell, William Crooke**; John Murray, London; first published 1903.

***** The Hornby Vellard**, is named for the British governor William Hornby who began it in 1782 as a project to unite all seven islands of Bombay into one with a deep natural harbor. It was completed in 1838.

Vellard is a corruption of the Portuguese *vallado* which means 'fence or embankment.'

Breach.' These were all ecologic assaults on the coast and the damaged ecosystem was primed to erupt in a tragic avatar — cholera.

Sealing-Wax

With the coming of cholera in 1819, the story of Bombay begins to blur. It is sucked now into the Imperial narrative of disease. It loses identity in the breathless rush of events as cholera is seen as a continuum from Calcutta to Ceylon, and British health officials give chase from town to town. The blame game begins elsewhere — in the Hejaz, in Alexandria, in Hamburg, in England.

Reportage of that time did not see beyond the giddying whirl of a disease that was yet to be understood.

At a remove of 200 years, and with so much new information at hand, isn't it time these reports were read as history, and not science?

Cabbages

The coastal strip of North Bombay has traditionally been the city's vegetable garden. Every housewife learns the most lush greens to be had are from Vasai. Bombay's vegetables find affectionate mention from European chroniclers starved of 'green stuff' at sea. The redoubtable Dr. Fryer swears that Bombay onions are sweet as apples.

Sadly, the present cannot keep pace with history. These gardens and orchards were traditionally watered by percolation wells. The demand of meeting Bombay's insatiable appetite has accreted grotesquely and boomeranged. Overuse and unwise exploitation has depleted the groundwater aquifer, upset the Ghyben-Herzberg equation and allowed saline intrusions, turning the water brackish and unfit to either drink or to irrigate.

Our island is solidified magma from the Deccan Traps

and our aquifers are perched, at varying depths, and our groundwater cannot travel. The entire Western Ghat is seismic and a geologic hotspot. The 1819 earthquake that formed the Allah Bund in Gujarat was felt throughout Bombay. It was also the year Bombay experienced its first outbreak of cholera.

Kings

Imperialism decided and sealed Bombay's fate in the 19th century. The consequence meant a frenzy of quarrying, deforestation, demolition and construction.

The railways were laid beginning 1850 and the Bombay-Thana link opened in 1853. Nagpur, Raichur and Ahmadabad were all soon connected. The first mill opened in 1851, and the Ghats were tunneled six years later. The docks came next — Mazagaon in 1866, Princess Dock in 1880, and Victoria in 1884.

Much of this was private enterprise and the investors were British and American. The objective was easier access and speedier transportation of cargo. Timber was free and labor cheap. The roads and railway were built by the starving and the destitute. And there were famines enough to guarantee a worker willing to walk ten miles and work twelve hours each day to take home 500 gms of rice.

And why the sea is boiling hot…

Over the last 125 years, global temperature has risen by 0.8°C. Polar icecaps are melting, glaciers recede every year, and permafrost, that obdurate layer which imprisons time itself, has begun to relent. These silent changes orchestrate the sound and fury of cyclones, floods, rains unseasonal and violent or else delayed, drought, famine, disease and death.

As the ocean heats up, thermal expansion of water raises sea levels. From 1910 to 1990, the rise was 1.5 mm/year, but between 1993 and 2003 sea levels rose at the rate of 3.5 mm/year.

These oceanic changes are inseparable from those on land. Greenhouse gas emissions are responsible for higher near-surface ocean temperatures, and sea levels are likely to rise faster than computed projections. The ice melt from the polar caps and Antarctica forces more CO_2 and methane into the atmosphere, to add to the fug from fossil fuels. Deforestation bares every continent and soon there will be too little green cover to take in all this CO_2.

There has been a 350% increase in the coastal phytoplankton bloom over the Arabian Sea since 1997 due to increased nitrates. This has been caused by upwelling from stronger southwest monsoons induced by a hotter Eurasian landmass which grows ever more deficient in snow cover.

The ocean teems with life forms that have exoskeletons of calcium carbonate. Think of what swimming in weak acid would do to them. And think of what it would do to us, afloat on soda, inhaling the pop.

...And whether pigs have wings

Diseases cannot always be prevented with vaccines and eradicated with drugs, not without payback. Yet that's all we seem to do every time. Till next time. With each new plague that hits us, we design prevention and cure all over again.

We need to look at plagues in an entirely different way.

ॐ

The Centrality of Wander in Creative Space

PRIYA SARUKKAI CHABRIA

ஐ

Parting

I was working on a story when the mood broke. Three of my friends had suddenly broken up with their partners. They began downloading on me over long phone calls, marathon e-mails, and face-to-face. True, I had invited this in some way; maybe it is my writer's greed for stories. But the listening became painful; the air turned into shiny needles that hurt with every breath.

Amid the choking rain of needles I sought for words which would comfort them but only saw the trauma. To each one I repeated that time would transform if not heal, and it's all for the better; and yet I felt hollow. Repeating the same phrases into the mirror of shock, into the well of sorrow, into the reflection of confusion.

Gradually they retreated, one by one, to their new lives. And once again I was left in the green calmness of my house with a broken story waiting within the endless pages

of my computer. Again I sought words and wrote this, to
grasp the air.

She Says to Her Friend:
He said to me: Keep faith.
So I kept a stubborn faith in him
which grew with every difficulty:
Swollen, taut, ready.
I held this close within myself feeling
his absent presence fill me
full, warm, moist.
Suddenly —
this small discharge,
for him a little thing.
His rapid pulling out
of me peels away my very skin.

The Centrality of Wander
I though of what it is to be a woman witnessing broken
relationships and bearing unfinished stories. How could
one hope again? This is when she crossed the horizon of
my mind, appearing on the brim of the liminal like the
glow of a firefly, drifting off and on: The *abhisarika nayika*
, an ancient icon of love in Sanskrit poetics abundant with
desire, profuse in interpretation.

She appears and reappears in our various art forms as
an image of transgression, desire embedded in her beautiful
form, always journeying, signifying a path beyond. In
several paintings she appears as a pale figure lighting the
fearful darkness of a stormy, demon-infested night. In other
paintings she could be tranquil as the moonlight through
which she journeys, resolved in her quest. Yet again she
could be carrying flower garlands as gifts for her secret
lover while each creature of the night is vivid with
expectation, rejoicing in her every step. Of course, the

outer landscape she traverses is a metaphor of the inner, within her frail, fast-beating heart.

In poems and legends she journeys across the forbidden to clandestinely meet her lover for a night of joy, her desire supreme. We can see her in sculpture, arms swaying; her body corroded by sunlight and touch yet alive with movement and passion. And in music and dance she rises with notes and words, with gesture and movement, with breath and improvisations to once again sing the song of rebellion, of refusing to be moored to social mores and conventions. She consistently walks through the centuries and the arts carrying with her the fragrance of difference.

Of course, she was also given religious signification. In the tradition of high aesthetics she personified the concept of the individual atma — the individual self — seeking out the Paramatma, the Absolute Consciousness; her overwhelming sexual yearning transmogrified to encompass a paramount desire for spiritual becoming. With the sky of longing cast over her the *abhisarika nayika* wanders as lover and seeker, the male always the beloved.

It is she who turns her back on the warm interiors of home to merge with the dark glow of forbidden desires; she sheds her earlier identity like a dupatta, like a veil, a miasma, uncovering deeper levels of self as her love deepens. It is she who stands parting veils of rain, which fall like teardrops, like pearls from a dark yet gracious sky, parting the rain, parting her fears from her desire. Hands reddened with tenderness, eyes lined black with hope, bejewelled by her own splendour she stands on the threshold of transfiguration.

She could be a noble woman or a cobbler's wife for the sweep of her wandering was not proscribed by a caste, a class, a tradition. Embodying unbounded passion for her secret love the *abhisarika nayika* is a construct contained within the predominantly brahminical and patriarchal codes of the Margi or Great Tradition. But unrestrained she changes her name, though not her transgressive character, and weaves just as freely through our many older Desi or Little Traditions — the folk, the tribal, the others — and her steps taking on the sensuous lilt of these landscapes. The plangent energy and lack of 'purity' in her construction speak of the constant overflow between the different traditions, and the colour of local culture. For the Margi and Desi Traditions have twisted around each other like copulating snakes, or strands of DNA that must be read together in order to make sense, be fecund.

Of Serpents and Stories

The overlapping and intertextuality of the *abhisarika nayika's* myth speaks of more than a fluid entwining between the traditions and the arts; it speaks of the ground from which it was birthed, the womb of the vision. This is of a polycentred universe were profusion and abundance are expressions of the underlying harmony of all life forms. It is this idea that has frothed over in the arts as profligate vitality of thought and gesture, as a swimming maze of multiple narratives and diverse interpretations that allow many points of view to be held concurrently without apparent contradiction.

This is why, initially, the form of many art works seems like liquid chaos. For there are multiple points of entry into paintings and even the margins of the frame can unfold parallel narratives. There is constant moving back and forth in the space-time of narrations and there are stories within stories, and asides. As if a thousand jeweled story-snakes are circling round and around in the lake of perception. Until one isn't sure which is moving, the snakes or the lake, or are they both static, and is the observer moving? Or in is the play something different?

For me, the wonder of the supple, generous creativity

of this subcontinent is its sustained plurality of form and interpretation. For instance, thousands of different versions exist of the epic, *Mahabharata*. As if there is there just one serpent in the lake that merely sprouted one more head on its many-hooded form to accommodate a newer version of the story while the various other heads continue to shake, spewing their contradictions while special jewels glitter on each hood.

This suggests we consistently live with simultaneous and multiple inconsistencies; and hypocrisy. And one questions how this slippery excess does not slid into a swamp of meaninglessness. At the risk of oversimplification (and this is ironic) I'd say it's largely because of context-sensitivity: The need to earth the narration within the specificity of resonance, ground it in a landscape of a particularity, an individuation of interpretation, a framing. In the essay *Is There an Indian Way of Thinking?* A K Ramanujan, poet and linguist, wrote, "In such a world, systems of meaning are elicited by contexts, by the nature (and substance) of the listener." Therefore, ten different tellings of the same story can exist side-by-side; possibly entwining at points, all reconcilable and specific to different truths.

Profusion and context sensitivity, these two paradigms operate simultaneously one on the other within the same space: Profusion as a window constantly opening outwards, and context-sensitivity as a mirror reflecting inwards, interlinking reflected stories, opening pathways into the dark margins of ellipses.

Fluid, multiple narratives, besides resonating with the concept of a harmonious, polycentric universe also play a crucial part in the reception of these narratives: They resist easy encoding. This occurs even though the narratives are themselves familiar as in the recurrence of the *abhisarika nayika* motif or numerous retellings of the *Mahabharata*.

For embedded into these narratives is not only the creative presence of the receiver, the *sahrdaya* , but also that of the storyteller or the painter or performer. The challenge for each artist during each recreation of the narrative is to give it a fresh luminosity, an apurva form, whereby the narrative is re-birthed in the mind of the receiver, making for a new layer of contemporary meanings. This continuous process of individuation and improvisation allows the stories and motifs to keep churning with each retelling, at each point in time, in each village and city.

For me, each myth and story holds its tail it its mouth like a great snake while simultaneously shedding its skin. It sloughs off the tight, confining skin of irrelevance, beneath the old body glimmers with fresh scales of light, ready for challenge. Once again soft with hope, it is plangent, vocal, free. It is no one's property.

These are forms of artistic expression to which I am committed, and which are being threatened in some quarters for there are snake charmers today who want to trap this treasure in small dank baskets of ideology, allowing it to rise only to the seduction of their tunes. Far worse, they want it enslaved for the venom it can spew if provoked in a certain direction, not for the jewels on its hood. And not a thought for its splendour, the coiling, fecund story-self.

The Return of the Abhisarika Nayika

Didn't we last see her standing on the threshold of transfiguration, sure only of her passionate love?

Her most vaulted avatar is as Radha, the older married woman who goes out into the forests of the night to meet Sri Krishna, her divine lover on the banks of the river Jamuna. She quietens her anklets so that her mother-in-law will not hear her, stills the bells on her girdle so as not to awaken her sleeping husband, and steps out in canto after canto in Jayadeva's *Gita Govinda*, written in the 12th century. But even in her avatar as Radha the *abhisarika nayika* has gradually been made more virtuous. The jagged, transgressive edges of her construction as the 'older married' woman have been elided so that she becomes a gracious consort, a gentle accessory to the Godhead. Today most often we see her in temples and shires in homes, carved of the same white marble as Sri Krishna, standing by his side and bestowing her lesser blessings on devotees.

The legacy of Radha and the many anonymous *abhisarika nayikas* is sporadic and transformed by commerce and religiosity. But the trail is decipherable even in our best-loved medium. In commercial films the love-call still occurs in the gardens, in sylvan settings of forests and glades, rarely indoors. The exquisitely dressed heroine, the 'good girl', still needs the ambience of the outdoors, the suggestion of transgressing the threshold of the home to declare herself in love — in order to live happily ever after indoors.

To return to Radha's stories I recall a conversation with a childless widow. She was a distant, elderly aunt, draped in the inauspicious white of North Indian widowhood, who related the story when I was a new bride so that I learn how to behave, now that I was indoors. In her version, Radha was a pubescent virgin, always 'pure' who devoted herself selflessly to her Lord; the relationship between them remained 'pure' throughout.

I remember contesting her version and causing a fair amount of violation. Now I doubt I would dispute the point with a widow who had possibly remained 'pure' herself throughout her wedded life. Moreover one needs to wander through the heady fragrance of difference and equanimity, through garden and forest, by the riverside, even through a desert if necessary, seeking the faint far-flowering of a cactus blossom.

Rub it Right: New Myths for Old

The genius of the local can often be translated into a dangerous selectivity when the fist of fundamentalist thinking closes in. A predominant local idea can be lofted and twisted as easily as a chiffon scarf in the wind to justify the twisted ease with which narrow and divisive factions gain power to stymie difference. Ironically, these minorities have 'imported' the context-free concept of Egalitarian democracy — with a twist. They accept the idea of a universalising law that speaks of one rule for all to override our uneven context-sensitivity. Thereby they claim sole access to an authentic and homogeneous 'Indian' culture. Wherein 'Purity' supplants profusion; One frozen Truth replaces the simultaneous living many.

"This is perversion of our culture, it's immoral foreign influence," they say and ban a book without reading it or stop the shooting of a film. "These are the vicious fallouts of globalisation, "they can assert elsewhere and no one is quite sure who is the next victim. Could it be the *abhisarika nayika* who journeys with her 'impure' burning heart of love? Or a concept of love, newly lit?

Burning Hearts

St. Valentine's Day has become a youth phenomenon even in our small towns; it is an unprecedented marketing coup for a globalized lifestyle; a gigantic gobble into the imagination and wallets of a spreading middle class. But let's look at it differently. As the latest addition to our list of celebrations for this civilisation is sometimes compared to a boa constrictor that has an amazing appetite for swallowing other cultural constructions and growing heavier, not falling ill. The Gregorian calendar's New Year has recently been co-opted. In many parts of the country on New Year's eve temples bustle with activity because the Gods have happily accepted this Western tradition in the old spirit of absorption. The priests, the flower and incense sellers, the coconut vendors and devotees are also happy.

Yet the survival capabilities of this ancient serpent are being questioned anxiously by the extreme rightwing that issue warnings that make front-page news. These organisations have decided they will work out an action plan to protect Hindu society against various forms of "cultural imperialism from the West," the most recent being Valentine's Day. Here is another quote that makes 'Indian' and 'Hindu' synonymous. "We are extremely concerned over the Valentine culture which has no roots in the Indian soil."

Not to be outdone, workers from a more liberal political party made bonfires at roadsides out of Valentine Day cards. I wondered what was burning, what is left. I thought of ash flakes hissing on roads of opportunism. All in the name of love.

Wings of Desire

It's ludicrous to champion the sale of cards that have tinsel-winged cupids, heart-shaped eggless chocolate cakes for veggie Valentines, synthetic linked-heart necklaces, twin-heart rings, frilly pink lace heart talismans, plastic red roses and syrupy verses. One does not wish to endorse market gluttony, nor cloying poetry.

Far worse, one doesn't wish to support the sexist agenda that's crept in to the celebrations for I am informed that the 'boys' must buy presents for the 'girls'. It's not reciprocal as it was once upon a time in my elitist collage, and we know disparity leads to grave disharmony between the genders.

It is obvious there can be no single perspective, nor easy consensus. But can one condone the juggernaut of multinational culture in order to resist a more immediate outburst that threatens the profusion and simultaneity of our culture? Is it possible to fly unhindered over these landscapes steering one's path of work by the luminosity of a serene moon? With what wings does one rise when all around there is antinomy and not life affirming plurality? Does context sensitivity have to give way to compromise and shrinking horizons? It's a truism that globalisation means different things in different climates and circumstances. Even so if one wishes to resist this cultural aberration one read with despair that on 14 February 2000 in the city of Kanpur bullies blackened the faces of celebrating couples.

What are the options, I wonder. How does one sprout wings of desire that even when spiralling downwards can transport us to tenderness?

Repossession

What does the wing-beat of the heart stir as it falls towards darkness if not the desire for generosity?

I ask myself about the apurva form, the new luminosity and re-contextualising I should return to the *abhisarika nayika* who has sustained me so generously.

I first try to imagine the final scenario, death, which illuminates living. In a flash she appears treading the threshold of a time when both inner and outer spaces must be profuse with meaning and slightness, more cherished yet spiralling towards The End. That journey into darkness, taking steps completely alone, transgressing all known modes of behaviour and ideology, when one is possibly full of fear, possibly remembering the passage through life and hoping for tranquillity, calm as distant moonlight. What could she embody here, I ask myself. Possibly courage?

But it is impossible to imagine that wing-beat of parting which must shock as each taut hope and position is pulled away. Till the very self is peeled away and absence reveals itself in an incomprehensible completeness.

What, then, does the *abhisarika nayika* embody as I question and love? What is her new interpretation? She is stripped of the significance of 'illicit' love and the grand fading echoes of an ultimate becoming. Yet she resonates with the yearning of absence, still stubborn, splendid, transgressive, wandering on wild paths that appear before her feet. She still carries flower garlands of hope and the darkness quickens with her fragrance of difference. What is this avatar of hers? Possibly the creative self journeying. No more. No less.

Kalabhairavan

T PADMANABHAN

ಕಾ

Translated from the Malayalam by
A J THOMAS

He was not sure when the sun had risen. For some months now, he had no worries about time. The night comes. And the day follows just like that. Everything was the same to him. The truth was that he had no watch on his wrist. He had been wearing the watch when he set out from home. It was lost somewhere during the journey. He had not particularly felt any inconvenience on account of losing his watch. For that reason, he had not thought about it ever again.

He had been sitting by the river, on the *pyol* of a structure built long ago by a king, but now mostly in ruins. There were such structures and temples in their hundreds on the river bank. But he didn't have much trouble in singling out this structure from among them. Iyer, the restaurant owner who had run away from home and found refuge at Kashi years ago when he found that life had reached a dead end, had told him: "Go over to Ramnagar, crossing the Ganga. You only have to walk along the riverbank. There, before you reach the palace of the king of Ramnagar... no, you will not lose your way. Whoever you ask to would show his *ashram*. There is nothing much of an *ashram* there. A *sadhu* who came from somewhere lives there. An old, mostly dilapi-dated structure. Just that you can't say it is an *ashram* in the ordinary sense..."

He was sitting on one of the stairs of Dashaswamedha Ghat one night, when it had turned quiet, after the people had left. Iyer, too, was at his side. The air carried the smell of a burning human body, from a pyre not very far off. On the calm Ganga waters free of waves, the moon's pale reflection was seen. "For Kashi, it is indeed a very quiet night by any standards..."

Iyer said: "I am not sure whether I can use the word *sannyasi* about him. Or, why should I air my opinion? You are an educated and well-informed person; and you have seen life, too. Go, meet him and decide for yourself. I feel you should have met him much earlier..."

He looked up at Iyer's face questioningly. I should have met him much earlier?

What for?

No, no...

So many of such meetings...

He said none of these things. Only looked up at Iyer's face. But his mind was set. As if divining it, Iyer said: "I am not an educated or experienced person. And I am conscious of that. Somehow I reached here. I had not left specifically for Kashi. But God willed it to be that way. I have seen so many types after I reached here — so many who live in God's name and make capital out of it. There were also famous ones among them. But I have never seen anyone like him. If you ask me what is so special about him, or what merits he has got, I will not be able to tell you. That's why I said, go and meet him yourself. In fact, I don't even know his name. Or, does he have a name? Even that's not certain. It is not long since he reached here in Kashi. And no one knows for how long he will be here..."

A human being!

Both of them had sat without saying anything. The pale moon had been mostly framed in a mist-halo by that time. The sky and the river were dark alike. There was no sound from anywhere. Iyer was gazing at the middle of the river as if following something flown down, some name-less thing. Although they were silent, it was clear that that silence was there not because they had nothing to talk about.

Out of the blue, Iyer asked: "Have you ever loved a girl? Ever... believing that you could marry her and make her your wife, and live together?"

He was startled. He had never expected such a question from Iyer. In their acquaintance of a few days, there had never occurred between them a conversation which could lead to such a question now. There had never even been a hint that Iyer would ask such a question. And he could not give a ready answer.

Again Iyer said: "...and have you loved that girl like your life, forgetting everything, caste and clan, family and the public? And has that love itself turned into a wildfire and consumed that girl? And... did you have to run away to escape from that fire?"

"No? I thought you were also a fugitive like me, who seeks to escape the effects of your *karma*. That, something like what happened to me must have happened to you as well. That, due to a momentary slip, something to grieve over for the rest of your life must have happened to you too. No?"

He could not come out with a reply.

His mind was deeply disturbed. Iyer said again as if to

him-self: "So far I haven't spoken to anyone about these things. Just take it that it is because I had not come across someone who seemed to be a fit person to talk to. And now I have talked... and you do not respond. No. No need to reply. So many years have gone by. I have never returned. There were occasions when I felt like returning. But, always at the last moment I desisted... No one came in search of me, ei-ther. At least, a few who chanced to see me here during these years must have recognised me. "Isn't he our *Ambi*?" But... but no one... Perhaps, to them I must be one who is counted among the dead. One who does not deserve to live... Or, why think about it all now..."

As Iyer went on laying open the baggage of the past, he main-tained silence, without interrupting him with questions or comments. At first, he had tried to listen to that story out of politeness. Iyer was the one who gave him shelter at Kashi. Besides that, he had felt a special respect for him from the time he met him. It was not merely the gratitude for getting food or a place to sleep at night. And yet, when Iyer began to speak about the most important event of his life — and for the first time ever — he could not concentrate for long. His mind flitted over several parallel incidents, in his own life and those of others.

And his mind flowed long back into the past, caught in the tor-rent of time. He was alone then, and disconsolate. Land was not any-where in sight, to rest upon for a while, knowing full well that it was going to be his last respite ever. But such a spot was non-existent.

Although he was sitting on one of Ganga's steps, beside Iyer, he was actually present at that moment in an alley, in a countryside in Kerala. A dark, deserted alley. He waited there impatiently. He knew that the girl would pass that way. So he waited. He didn't hear the drumbeats of the temple feast; he was listening to the drumbeats of his own heart. All *asuravadya*s beat loudly and in great tempo. As he was caught up by the clamour of that drumbeat, she arrived finally.

Was she frightened seeing him there at that hour? She must have been. That's why she tried to turn around and run. But he blocked her escape route. He had once seen a live tree in full blaze after a bolt of lightning had struck it, in the pelting rain of the month of *Karkidakam*. The deluvian rain, thunderclaps, lightning. The tree standing still and burning alive, without being able to run away to safety. He was also more or less like that tree at that moment. Burning alive!

She had looked at his face only once. She said in fear: "Leave me, leave me alone..."

At first he was at a loss for words. Then, he said with much difficulty: "No."

Time froze before them.

A few moments later he said: "I want to know something for certain, not whether you love me, nor whether you are coming away with me. What I want to know is whether what I hear is true. You..."

"What? To learn the truth about what?"

He said what he had heard; his mind was then filled more with pain than with anger. As for himself, the whole foundation of a life he had dreamed of had been collapsing. It was because he wanted to escape from this situation that he asked her thus. He yearned to hear her say: "No. What you heard is not true." He would have forgiven everything if she said so. To reestablish that bond which he believed was never severed, he would have done anything.

As he looked at her face expectantly, she said: "You, you, I..."

He was powerless to hear it completed. Before he knew what was happening, he had...

He was stupefied.

What had he done?

Stupefaction turned into fear. Later on it turned into remorse. Although fear passed quickly, he couldn't get out of remorse. The more he thought about it, it ate him up like fire on chaff..."

Where-all had he wandered with that weight in his heart! Where-all!

Did he get his release?

Did he get his salvation?

As it was nearing midnight, Iyer said: "Come, let us go... It' quite late. I said so many things. And you said nothing."

Getting up, he scooped up water from the river and washed his face. When the cold water struck his face, he cried out inadvertent-ly: "Oh mother!"

He was about to turn back, when suddenly he felt that a man was crouching at the corner of the stairs! When he strained his eyes, he thought he saw another person also beside him. A woman! On Ganga's shores, at midnight, a young man and his...

That girl was weeping, he thought. Sobbing away...

Suddenly a thought crossed his mind like a meteor.

Jagannatha Panditan!

The one who created *Ganga Lahari*...

Goose-pimples rose all over his body.

He could not put a further step forward.

Jagannatha Panditan! The one who declared to his community that he would not forsake the girl he loved — that, too, a girl belonging to a different community! They who — when confronted with the reality that the two of them could never marry and live as husband and wife, when every door in Kashi was shut in their face — found their final refuge in the Ganga that endures all! Mother, here we come. We have nowhere else to go. Accept us. We have no one else but you Mother... none...

Thumping his back, Iyer asked: "What... what is it?"

He pointed towards the corner of the stairs.

When Iyer flashed the torch, there was no one.

He said softly: "I saw something!"

Iyer looked at him sharply. "You are imagining things; it is because of your fear. Fear of the court and the police. Now that you have reached Kashi, nothing will happen to you."

When Iyer said it to console him, he never told Iyer it was not for fear of the police or the court that he had left home or even that he had never committed homicide although it could well have ended in that, and in truth it was his own mind that he was afraid of and it was from this mind he wanted refuge, and that he was trying to attain it. And he thought Iyer wouldn't understand either, if he said all that. So when Iyer talked, he just listened.

But he promised Iyer that he would go and meet, without much delay, the *sannyasi* living somewhere on the way to Ramnagar.

They returned to the restaurant through the deserted streets of Kashi. Iyer went on talking. But in his mind there were only the paths he had left behind and the people he had come across. When they reached back at the restaurant and he lay down to sleep, his mind was inhabited by them. Then, as usual, there were the thoughts about the inevitability of the results of one's *karma,* and the delicate line dividing the right and the wrong.

Before he was fully enfolded in the embrace of sleep he said to himself: "I shall go... yes. I shall go and meet that *sannyasi,* too, who lives on the way to Ramnagar. How many have I met! And how many more..."

So it was thus that he set out on the morrow...

There were only the two of them — he and the *sannyasi* — on the *pyol* of that dilapidated structure. The *sannyasi* did not wear any of the outward vestiges of *sannyas,* like saffron, matted hair or beard. He was sitting, but not in any particular *asana,* looking at the sun behind the mist. He sat on folded legs on bare floor. There was no deerskin or leopard skin to sit on.

The *sannyasi* had not closed his eyes. Yet, it was doubtful whether he had seen him sitting in front, concentrating all attention on him.

Then he began to recite softly...

"Heh! Chandrachooda Madananthaka Soolapane
Staano Gireesa Girijesa Mahesha Sambho!
Bhootesa! Bheeta Bhayasootana Mananatham,
Samsaaradhukhgahanajjagadisha raksha!
Heh! Parvathi hridaya..."

(O wearer of the crescent moon
Destroyer of the god of Love
Holder of the spear, Lord of the mountains,
Lord of the Lady born to the Mountain, Great
Lord!
Lord of Ghosts, who removes the fear of the frightened
Save us, O Lord of the Universes, from *samsara*
dukha.
O Lord of Parvathi's heart...)

He listened to it in rapt attention in a childlike wonder. He was not hearing those *slokas* for the first time. He had heard his grandmother recite them in his childhood. Also other *slokas* like them. In his childhood, he too had recited them sometimes, together with his grandmother.

But this...

He stood there in a nameless wonder. Gradually the *sannyasi's* voice began to rise and spread to all directions and soon to reverber-ate from those directions. At that moment, he lost all awareness of time and space.

What he saw when he came around was the *sannyasi* smiling at him lovingly. The *sannyasi* beckoned to him to speak. Although he had so many things to say, he was unable to say anything.

The *sannyasi* stood looking at him. That gaze, although affection-ate, went deep into his mind like a dagger.

He felt as if he was turning naked.

Later the *sannyasi* asked him, as if remembering something: "Why did you come to Kashi at all?"

Then he replied: "I did not come here on my own. I just drifted in here."

The *sannyasi* nodded as if to say that he understood.

After a brief spell of silence, the *sannyasi* spoke to him about *karma,* its effects and the inevitability of it all and also about human beings who harbour illusions about trying to escape it. When the *sannyasi* stopped talking he said: "Isn't it my story?"

"May be. But, it is not your story alone; it's the story of everyone... everyone."

When he stood agape the *sannyasi* said as if to himself: "This is Kashi — Kalabhairavan's land. Kalabhairavan, who severed Brahma's head as he could not tolerate Brahma's lie. Kalabhairavan, who, on becoming aware of his guilt, wandered all over the universe in remorse and carrying the severed head in his hand. Kalabhairavan, who pondered over the right and the wrong, *papam* and *punyam,* over a long time. Kalabhairavan got his release from the effect of his *papakarma,* it is believed. People come here to wash away their sins. I don't know whether they are able to do it. I am not sure. Kalabhairavan could do it. That doesn't mean that even I can do it. We have to find our own Kashis... during this lifetime itself."

Looking at the sun beginning his climb towards the zenith, and at the shimmering watery expanse of the Ganga, the *sanny-asi* exclaimed in an awesome voice filled with grandeur: "Shiva! Shiva! Shiva!"

Then, walking through the cluster of boats pulled up on the sands, the *sannyasi* vanished. Though at first he thought of accompa-nying him, he didn't do so.

Sometime later, he, too, left the spot. But it was not for Kashi that he left.

।

Note: *asauravadya* — percussion instruments

Gone Away

KANKANA BASU

൬

Recently, an eighty-two-year-old man lay dying in the far suburbs of Bombay. In an advanced stage of respiratory failure, his anxious eyes strayed ever so often to the doorway to check whether his NRI son had arrived. When he finally passed away, the anguished gaze of the dying man continued to be fixed on the doorway, for a last look at his only son. The son arrived thirty-six hours too late and was met with cold rage from his relatives; whereupon he burst into noisy tears. The disapproval of the extended family was totally justified but the tears of the son were also all too real.

In another part of Bombay, an attractive spinster in her late forties travels to work every morning. The only daughter of a frail eighty-six-year widower, evenings are spent being caregiver to her sick father. Weekends are generally devoted to accompanying her father to the doctor and buying domestic provisions. Though she dreams of having her own home and family some day, marriage she knows, could tip the fragile balance. The only welcome interruption in her humdrum existence is the yearly visit from her US-settled married brother.

Is there a connection between these two arbitrary stories, you may well wonder. There is, dear reader, there is. In both cases the forlorn conditions of the octogenarian and the spinster are an offshoot of inadequate arrangements made by a vital family member who chose to settle abroad. As generations of youngsters lured by the prospect of fat pay-packets, better working conditions and an improved lifestyle move westwards, they often leave behind dependents at the mercy of a turbulent society. Look around and one is likely to see entire ghost colonies where the average resident is a citizen in his silver years struggling to cope. It is the inherent quality of magnanimity typical of this country, which encourages a protective streak in people who are always willing to lend a helping hand to the elderly and prevent him from being crushed under the juggernaut that is Bombay city.

Thus, when it comes to the visit to the doctor, shopping for groceries, banking or running from pillar to post-office for the legalities of survival, it is generally extended family, service attendants like postmen, peons, watchmen and the friendly neighbourhood shopkeeper who proxy for family. But like all other things, this phenomenon could be a double-edged sword, often laying the elderly open to all kinds of criminal intentions. The sharp rise in assaults on the city's elderly in recent times only illustrates this point rather harshly.

As thousands of graduates leave for foreign lands in search of greener pastures, there is a disturbing rise in parent-child estrangement. What are the factors responsible for this, wonder worried social scientists, as there appears to be no clear-cut solutions to the burgeoning problem. Psychologists in the city feel that it would be unfair to lay the blame squarely at the door of the children. Parental expectations and family pressures are often so stifling for a youngster that all he wants to do on graduating is get the hell out of the country and get a life of his own. On settling abroad, the parents are duly taken over for their yearly vacations but after a while, the daunting prospect of footing medical bills (always an exorbitant affair in a foreign land) and the traditionally-attired folks in their saris, *salwar*s, *bindi*s, *dhoti*s, chewing *paan* and proclaiming their Asian origins to all and sundry are a tad embarrassing for the NRI who is, in all likelihood, trying hard to blend in with the local flavour.

Likewise, the regular and enthusiastic visits of children to their homeland seem to gradually lose charm as the immunity-challenged NRI finds himself succumbing to the dust, noise and pollution of this city and baulking at the haphazard style it functions. He would prefer to holiday in exotic locations, spending the bare minimum in his homeland. In stray cases, when NRI children would genuinely like to relocate their parents to live close to them, it is often the elderly folks who are unwilling to leave familiar surroundings. And thus we have a stalemate situation which leads to a classic case of continental drift of the emotional kind.

An NGO worker recalls an incident where an irate young man who was urgently summoned home for his father's hernia surgery, turned and barked at his father. "Why can't you be as independent as the Americans? My ninety-year-old widowed neighbour in San Fransisco lives all on her own!" The recouping father sadly refrained from reminding his son how he had spent his entire savings to give him an expensive education besides forgoing many a personal luxury. A recurrent and regrettable trend in recent times, a huge number of youngsters are content to follow the traditional method when it comes to getting their education funded by parents but come payback time, they find it so much more convenient to adopt the Western system. The 'A' word hangs large and ugly on graying heads but the elderly prefer to bluff their way out by faking pride in their NRI children's achievements rather than admitting to a feeling of being 'abandoned'. A corollary to this filial estrangement is detachment from extended family, another recent trend with the younger generation refusing to bond with cousins, uncles, aunts and grandparents. The next-gen would prefer to opt out of family gatherings, networking sites and peer groups fast replacing extended family. With a predominance of single-child families, a bleak future of collapsing family structures seems imminent for this insulated lot, worry social scientists.

The law, or the lack of it, is partly responsible for their plight, agree senior citizens unanimously. The most intricate of laws have been formulated to ensure that a deceased parent's wealth and assets are distributed judiciously, with new rules banishing gender and marital-status biases popping up all the time. In contrast, there is hardly a solid body of laws that protect the rights and dignity of an ageing parent. Abandonment, harassment, physical and mental abuse or being thrown out of one's rightful home are often left to be dealt with at the local police station. So while children stand poised to inherit every asset garnered by their parents over a lifetime, parents stand doomed to an inheritance of loss.

The elderly, we have to periodically remind ourselves, make up not a just a section of society defined by sagging flesh and creaking bones but embody the storehouse of a country's tradition, culture, intellect and professional expertise, honed over decades. Can a country that claims to be shining really shine on unless it ensures pride of place to its senior citizens? A couple of visionaries are seeking to remedy the situation by building colonies exclusively for the elderly. NGOs for the aged, magazines aimed at a mature readership and a section of the celebrity world are trying to pitch in and do their bit for the silver citizens but it simply isn't enough. All efforts add up to make a minimal difference in the life of an average senior citizen living in Bombay.

The recent recession has brought about some welcome changes and a reversal of the brain-drain situation seems to be happening. Generation Long Lost is feeling the tug of tradition once again. With the big fat Indian family that has never hesitated to step in and assist in times of pink slips, financial downfalls and adversity on the horizon, the Westernised Indian is rediscovering his roots. But the India he is coming back to is far different from the country he left decades back and it may take a while for the two identities to step in sync with each other once again. But never mind the little hiccups, feel folks on both side of the ocean jubilantly, it's well worth the effort! The return of the prodigal spells hope to many as the bottom line for society is spelled out clear and sharp. No future cannot be effectively carved without acknowledging history and we can only move forward if we nurture the past.

Godhuli

(Cowdust)

TABISH KHAIR

Beyond the bend there were buffaloes,
Cows and a single boy perched,
Half-naked, on the back of a buffalo.
It was the twilight hour of cowdust.

Suddenly the angle of a woman's arm
Collecting cowdung cakes by the roadside
Made clear this blended hour, a word
That had nestled like a bird in my soul,
Made clear the dungsmoke swathed
Outlines of a mud village, its cowdung-
Smeared walls and floors, clarified
A whirl of cows. Our driver honked,
Scattering some. Others continued
Their slow, swaying walk across the road.
We inched through a gap in the herd,
Wreathed in cowdust, headlights switched on,
Casting faint, elongated shadows of cows
On this world of dust a word could touch.

Freedom

SHREEKUMAR VARMA

They came for him in the morning.

He had eaten indiscriminately, leaving his stomach a heavy, alien thing. Appu noticed his tension. "Be brave, Vijayan, nothing will be the same."

He knew that. "And you — don't forget to visit us when you're out." He pretended to be busy going over his things, weighed down by a sudden jump of pity and revulsion. He had grown used to the sprawling hall with its concrete bunks, these men.

Boots on the floor, their low-enquiring voices, the key in the lock, and this time it was his turn. He felt himself grow pale. Visit us? Why had he said that?

He heard a sullen voice. "What's wrong with him? Doesn't want to go or what? It's a remission, man, thinks he's off to the gallows!"

Down the long narrow passageway, their footsteps echoing. He sat down in the anteroom, waiting for Kuriakose. A warder sat with him, polishing his short fat *lathi* with the infinite patience of his job.

He could see into the office room behind the half-doors,

the newly-painted green walls, a red phone and dusty books. Kuriakose would take his own sweet time. A peon went in and out of the office clutching files, humming a film song. After a while, the doctor and a policeman passed by, talking in low voices. The warder tapped betel nut on his palm. After chewing for a while he inserted a finger into his mouth, probing.

There were too many shadows in here. He felt comfortable and a little drowsy. When he thought about it ten years was too much, too fast. In the beginning days stretched without hope. Then a routine set in. Everything by the bell. Assembly, exercise, workroom, classes, prayer. Once a week, work at the quarry. He looked forward to the outing. The sky was warm and infinite. After a week of closed spaces, the sound of metal on hot stone rang around the earth. It was hard work, with a scent of freedom.

The men inside had nothing to share but their past. When letters came, they sat around.

"*Ayyo* Vijayan, still nothing from her! Don't worry, women are like that. Let her see you once, she'll melt like butter." "Look at mine, different problem. She waits with fire in her belly!" "You fellows think I'll get back my job? I can't bear to be unemployed." "God have mercy, how many more months. Seven years since I saw my beloved two. They're both doing well in school. God bless!" "Your daughter's periods have started?" "Pah! Who are you, her grandmother? Asking about periods and all!"

Like Appu, he too was a sympathetic listener. He helped out in the workroom and infirmary, read aloud newspapers. Appu was older by several years. He had stopped a man from becoming a rapist. "I stopped him with these very hands." Some nights he woke up shouting: "It's a mistake!" Vijayan sat with him, trembling, helping him through the rest of the night. After hearing that he couldn't have slept anyway.

He was sweating. He bent to wipe his face with his shirtfront. The warder glanced at him. He had funny square eyes that pinned you down. "What's the matter?" Vijayan shook his head. The warder scratched his thigh robustly. "You waited so many years. A couple of hours won't kill you."

He leaned his head against the wall, idly rubbing his clean-shaven face with his fingers. There was a beard once. It had labelled him Scholar, like the cloth bag over his shoulder. Cobwebs floated lazily from the ceiling. This anteroom was a bridge to freedom. It was also the room where men sweated before an audience with Kuriakose. He didn't trust life. You could dream all you wanted but finally some cruel twist sank you. Chewed up and finished like a dog's bone. He no longer dismissed destiny. He had been a rationalist, seeking answers in the here and now, in action and determination. Life had changed him.

He tried to shut it out. He couldn't shut out her face. The men sympathised with him, saying she needed time to get used to the idea, of course she'd visit. They had lists of loved ones daunted by the idea of prison; it was a natural reaction. Vijayan listened in silence, unable to take their empty optimism.

His fingers remembered his beard. He'd been full of labels then, an intellectual with Marx sitting on his shoulders. Most of his classmates found Law a conduit to politics. His aim was to open a legal cell in his village for those who couldn't afford to fight injustice. He was an enigma. Idealism like this had died in the sixties.

It was this that attracted Meera. She was small and fragile, but a fire raged within her. Everyone knew how she'd slapped a senior in full view of the college, wrenching from the men for weeks afterwards their right to shout obscene comments. There had been no retaliation. She was like that.

They met as opponents, pitting wits at debates, mock courts and elocution contests. They hated, respected and scorned each other. Their confrontations puzzled their friends because they kept returning for more. One day someone wisecracked: "If you two ever got married, imagine the fighters you'd raise!" He replied, looking straight at her: "As long as they're standing up for the truth."

Antagonism drew them closer. Finally they discovered they were fighting for the same things from different corners. They sat in the library, in the canteen, under the mango tree behind the science block. Their discussions were intense, their silence powerful. They were mocked. "*Chhe*, what a romance! At this rate they'll read Contracts to each other on their wedding night!" But conversation was a bond; romance had nothing to do with it.

She stayed in a small, rented house on the outskirts. Her father was a retired journalist. One day she took Vijayan home to meet him. The visit was a revelation. Her father turned out to be VPN whose courageous writings and Leftist convictions had shaped him through his adolescence. All three were surprised. Meera had never realised the extent of her father's influence. The old man thought people had forgotten him.

He hardly spoke a word. Respectfully he watched them in their roles as father and daughter, surprised by this supremely talented family. He saw old photographs of a sprightly bearded VPN spattered on the walls, speaking at college functions, meeting politicians, inaugurating political forums and showing solidarity with workers, farmers and tattered squatters. There was a feeling of speed, as though he was rushing through events like a runner who has to stop. The shelves were lined with slim volumes, the large magical *VPN* glowing on their spines, and bound collections of his articles. An era of political inspiration lived on in that room.

Vijayan held his tongue. He wanted to, but couldn't talk about Venu, his eldest brother killed in a police encounter seven years ago. He lay in hospital for three days before he died. His last words were: "Let the Master know."

Did the Master know? It was doubtful. With the grief in the house and the constant tension of police interrogations, no one would have found the time to inform VPN. Venu was martyred in the Master's name without the Master even knowing. Vijayan spent months in mourning and confusion, on the verge of hating VPN for leading his brother to sudden death.

The books made up his mind for him. Venu had accumulated a library, and VPN had the pride of place. He was barely into his teens when he began reading his books and articles.

They weaved a spell around him. They gave him a philosophy to sustain his life. While others spouted fire, VPN alone shed light. He was aware and kind. It was a difference that transformed Vijayan's thinking. VPN wrote: "Before you think of your own livelihood, consider the lives of others."

Even afterwards, when the rest of the world abandoned the Master, Vijayan remained true, bathed in an afterglow, the sputtering tail of a vanishing comet. He strode through school and college, part of a team of three, staunchly supported by his dead brother and the spirit of VPN.

But now it seemed a long story to be telling them. He checked himself, listening instead. As he left the house, the old man said, "Come again. I don't get too much company." He brooded over these words. A man like him. Did he long for company? Why weren't youngsters flocking to him?

After that day, his attitude changed. She was heir to the wisdom of the Master. Now their closeness could no longer conceal their feelings. Classmates teased them mercilessly.

It angered them, but they still didn't recognise the fuel they were adding to the fire.

One Sunday afternoon he went to see her father. He was laughing to himself. It was what their classmates had seen months ago. Through all their cheap taunting had emerged a truth that now struck him like a sunburst.

He wished he could gauge her feelings. From opponents they'd grown into friends, but did she feel anything more?

VPN reclined in his armchair, watching television. It was amusing, the great VPN watching a mushy Malayalam serial. "You like watching these things?" he asked. VPN smiled and switched off the set. "There are very few things left for me." Vijayan felt something freeze. Age had robbed this man of his robustness, a certain edge. "Why don't you write?"

The old man laughed and shook his head. He changed the subject, saying his daughter was out with friends, so would he make tea for both of them. Vijayan felt flattered, welcomed into the inner sanctum of their house. They sat out in the tiny veranda with their coffee. Vijayan tried to get him to speak about his past, his writings and his early motivations. It was a warm day with a good breeze. They could hear birds and squirrels from the trees in the neighbouring compound. The fish-vendor's peculiar call, a loud lowing whistle, petered off as the man cycled away.

"There's no more reason to write," VPN said.

It was the most extraordinary statement. Vijayan sat on the parapet, leaning against the wall. The empty coffee cups were in front of him. VPN was bunched up in a wooden chair, his knees drawn up sharply to his chin. No reason to write! At first he thought VPN was joking. Vijayan was besieged by the feeling that he'd intruded into some weakness of the old man.

VPN spoke about his daughter. He seemed concerned about her future. "What can a motherless girl find in this town?"

"She's a brilliant girl, sir. She'll have no problem finding her way."

VPN laughed. "Brilliance cannot lead your life for you."

The sunlight grew brighter and brighter.

A month later, swallowing his bewilderment, he visited again. He had avoided Meera in college, not knowing how to face her. His state of mind was reflected in a dream where he sailed on a large steamer with lots of people and things to do, and there was a feeling of togetherness and a sense of purpose, and the waters were way below, a swirling untouchable mass. In the dream he went to sleep in his bunk, staring out of the porthole at the brilliant stars in the black sky, and when he woke up next morning he was on a raft right in the lap of a rough sea, tossed and screaming and waiting for the end.

That evening VPN took out a bottle of toddy and two glasses. Meera withdrew into her bedroom, saying, "I don't disturb him." VPN explained: "It sometimes takes the edge off old age." Vijayan politely declined a drink and watched him down two bottles and turn into a garrulous, slightly boastful raconteur. Mosquitoes harassed them in the stuffy inner room. Vijayan felt a strong desire to get away, to escape into the night.

Instead, he listened to stories of courage and daring, sympathy and honour, of celebrities the old man had met, issues he'd tackled. He was being guided through an era where something mattered all the time, when your time was never your own.

Slowly, Vijayan relaxed. But later when he declared his admiration, the old man smiled and shook his head. "I was being paid to write. Like an actor who plays his part. What to do, the novelty wears off and you return to your own life. With responsibilities and problems."

The conversation progressed. Vijayan felt a deep disappointment. It was a terrible, unreachable facet of history. VPN's idealism had gradually ebbed until finally it remained a mere tool to earn a livelihood. He'd lived in a time of vigour and struggle; he was a product of the times. But like so many others, he had succumbed to the dreary requirements of ritual living, of prescribed reactions and inevitable consequences.

VPN! That three-letter magic had remained only in the minds of his admirers. His own reality had sucked him into its miserable depths like quicksand. The world outside was simply an office or workshop where he was paid to write, lecture and advise. Vijayan felt his dream blister and wither. The old man's voice droned on.

My brother was betrayed. He clenched his teeth and wished he knew what to do.

VPN said, "I'm glad I was able to influence so many youngsters. Youth needs the romance of ideals." Vijayan stared. Was the drink dredging up the true VPN?

He didn't personally believe anything he wrote! Vijayan was shocked. *You deceived an entire generation of youngsters!*

The night wore on. VPN lowered his voice. "I don't want her to hear but my girl is a source of great worry. It's time she thought of settling down, getting married."

"What about her Law?"

"She's a woman, does all that matter?" He sat brooding. "Already people are talking. Things would have been different if her mother were alive. Everyone blames me for her plight."

"What plight?" The words rushed out before he could stop them, like a spray of anger.

"She's twenty. Should she be in Law College, or getting married and having children?"

"She'll get a degree and do something good with her life."

VPN continued to shake his head. "Who'll let her continue her studies? Where can we find such a husband?"

Was that what made up his mind? Or did anger speed up his decision?

Abruptly, Vijayan held out his hand. "Just a second." Having got the old man's attention, he presented himself as the bridegroom who'd allow her to study. "As much as she wants!" VPN blinked, then waved him to silence. "Come tomorrow, we'll talk about it. This is not the time." The rest of the evening he drank hard, finished the bottles, sent him out to get a last one. As he left, VPN patted him on the shoulder. "Good boy!"

He couldn't sleep. His brother appeared in his dream, sweating and bleeding. *Why, Why? That man killed me!*

The next evening VPN spoke earnestly. He told Vijayan about his poor health. His motherless daughter was everything to him — son, daughter, mother. He would happily welcome Vijayan as his son-in-law.

He should have been happy. He wanted to break the news to her. Instead, he walked out frowning and disturbed. There was a sense of distaste, a feeling that grew like a poisonous vine, a little every day, wrapping around his heart, brain and nerves.

The man was as weak as his daughter was strong. He needed her support as he limped through his tepid life! VPN had a stroke behind him; he firmly believed a second, final one was waiting around the corner. "Today he's Master of self-pity!"

Many great men succumb to ordinariness once their provocations are done, when they reach an age that doesn't support their rage. But VPN had spent a greater part of his life playing a part. Except for the very early days, as a firebrand in the vanguard of the Left's greatest triumphs — except for that, VPN had been an actor! Playing the role of a hero to earn his keep.

Meera didn't know the feelings he harboured about her father till one day the dam broke. Venu and his death. His passion for VPN's writings, and the great need to meet him. And then the anti-climax!

She was pained by his ambivalence. She loved her father. Her idealism had been fuelled by him. Vijayan was over-reacting. "Think of the hundreds of people who still respect him," she said, almost pleading.

One day there was a *hartal* in the city, no traffic, shops, offices, no college. The local reading room was shut, but regulars were allowed to come in through the back. There were surprised to find each other. A couple of college girls, some old men reading newspapers, there was a silence in the hall like a shadow cast by the empty day. She was behind the racks looking for a book. He was reading. The hall emptied without their realising it, and they were alone.

He went to find her. She was kneeling, immersed in a fat volume, a pile of books on the floor beside her. She looked so vulnerable, so beautiful, he couldn't bear the distance between them and took her in his arms.

She threw a quick look over her shoulder but they were hidden from the librarian by the shelves. They had never been intimate before. She didn't protest as he crushed her in his embrace. He could feel his fingers scathing her soft skin.

He heard a sound and started to turn. Something hard hit him on the side of his head. She pushed him away and tried to get up, handicapped by the pile of books beside her. The pain throbbed, swelling his temple. He squinted from his sudden blindness and saw a group of boys, smirking.

"Breaking the *hartal* Love-making in the library, eh?"

His blood boiled. He heard her sob, a dry, painful sound. "Bastards!" he shouted. She clutched his arm, warning him to be careful. He had never seen her so vulnerable.

"What you think, this is bloody brothel or what?"

He heard a sound and saw the librarian peering timidly from behind a wall of books.

"Let's go," she whispered, trying to get up again.

"Hey you, can we also play this game? You want some real men? Wait at home today midnight, eh? We'll come for you!"

He heard her gasp. He saw the librarian's bulging eyes. When he looked again they had disappeared, their threat still echoing in the room.

The peon emerged from the shadows with two tumblers of coffee. The warder took both and handed one to Vijayan. The hot watery liquid scalded his tongue. He blew gently and watched the vapour rise. After a while, the warder said, "Come, I need a smoke."

They stood between the office building and the passageway. The warder lit a cigarette, handed one to him. He inhaled the smoke deeply. His hand was trembling. On the other side of the low wall, the prisoners had assembled for their drill. One of them issued sharp commands to the others. A couple of policemen lounged around, rifles hanging from their shoulders. He spotted Appu in the back row.

"This is what I'm leaving behind… and outside? Those eyes will haunt me forever. And the question will always follow me wherever I go. Was it really a mistake? Or were you right?" He clenched a fist to stop the trembling.

That night the three friends who shared the house with him went to see a late-night movie. He stayed back. But he couldn't sleep. He locked all the doors and windows and paced the front room like a caged animal. A madness seemed to have gripped him. He could still hear the words: "Wait at home at midnight. We'll come for you!"

To calm himself he picked up a book at random. The words made no sense. He drank several glasses of water. He couldn't forget the look in her eyes, the first time he'd seen her so vulnerable. He swung open the front door, took a few turns outside the house. Everything was silent in this late hour. The cool air, scented with flowers of the night, washed over him bolstering his purpose.

He opened Mohan's cupboard and took out his hockey stick. It was a quarter past eleven. He locked the house, left the key in its usual hiding place between the doorframe and the rafter, and walked out. He walked slowly but with determination. Stray stalkers of the night, a few cars and trucks, a parade of dogs jealously guarding the street. Some of them must have wondered. Who plays hockey here at night? But hockey sticks several uses. The stalkers kept a safe distance.

Their neighbourhood was deserted. The houses looked pale and unreal, like a ghost settlement. The sudden screech of a night bird startled him. He gathered his wits and sat down on a small cement slab just inside the wall. He leaned against the wall, prepared for a long vigil. Minutes passed. He could actually feel the sluggishness of time. He was tired and uncomfortable, there were mosquitoes above and ants below, wreaking unreasonable vengeance on him. The silence was unnerving.

He didn't know when he fell asleep. Some sound woke him up, a shout or a cry, human or otherwise. The sides of his mouth felt gritty, his eyes burned. His body ached with the cold hardness of its perch. He jumped to his feet. What was that sound?

And then he saw a figure hurrying away, down the side of the house. It was the figure of a man, thin, a towel wrapped around the head. He wanted to yell out, to make him stop, but the words wouldn't come out, his tongue felt swollen. The words echoed in his head: "Midnight! We'll come for you!"

He charged forward, the stick clutched painfully in his hand. The figure with the towel around the head was now coming back. Vijayan could hardly make out the man from the shadow. He yelled and raised the stick high, holding it with both hands. The figure cried out. He heard the sound distinctly, though he couldn't make out what was being said. He brought down the stick with all his strength. "Bastard!" Vijayan yelled.

Once was enough. The figure lay immobile, an untidy bundle grown from the ground. The moon came out. The moon had to come out then. To display his folly to himself in full brightness. A cruel imitation of a human being, the features tight with pain.

He couldn't move, the stick wouldn't drop from his hands, his legs were weakening horribly. He couldn't stop himself. The words poured out from him. Unstoppably. "It's a mistake, it's a mistake, it's a mistake—"

Later she said, "My father cried out. Even I heard that." The fire in her eyes was unmistakable.

The peon ran up. "Kuriakose sir has come."

The warder turned to Vijayan. "Okay, your time has come."

Appu and the others were still in the yard. Exercising briskly. Getting the sun. Obeying orders. Every minute of their time was accounted for. No decisions to be made, no relationships to be mended, no guilt. Most of all, no guilt. This was the place that cleaned up your guilt. He was leaving, walking away from here.

There was life in the games yard. In comparison, the office building looked forbidding, darkly grim.

Reluctantly he began to follow the warder.

છ

Lives of the Wise

ANJANA BASU

At the end of a book launch when the mike is passed around for questions and the hands reach out eagerly, there is inevitably one kind of question that crops up: "What are your thoughts on the terrorism issue. Do you feel it was linked to Partition?" "Would you like to comment on India's nuclear policy?" The questions may vary but the drift is fairly similar — the author by writing a book has shown that he or she is a person of substance and therefore equipped to deal with any kind of issue from politics to State Governance.

Perhaps this is the result of the awe engendered by anyone who can produce a work of art. It implies a superior kind of grey matter at work and India since time immemorial has respected grey matter. However, what is new and is possibly one of the weaknesses of the millennium is a rising belief that artists can lead double lives as activists.

Arundhati Roy is of course the best example of this — from *God of Small Things* she has moved on to involving herself with issues like the Narmada Bachao Andolan, anti-industrialisation in Bengal, Orissa, and protests against Indian brutality in Kashmir. The result has of course been several books of essays based on her op-ed pieces in foreign and Indian publications and a lot of media excitement which at least has engendered debate on the causes with which she has been associated with.

In Bengal the other example which over the past few years has been gaining prominence is that of the *budhijibi*s involved by Trinamul Congress leader Mamata Banerjee in her political campaigns. The wise lives who have been making headlines by clustering together to advise and protest.

In Bengal the intellectual activism coming to the forefront became headlines with Nandigram. On the 14th of March 2007, 14 people were gunned down at a crossing in the blaze of day sending a village called Nandigram in West Bengal onto the front page of every paper in India. The numbers were not meant to be coincidental, nor was the shooting planned. It was meant to be a peaceful protest where members of the Trinamul demonstrated against a proposed buyout of agricultural land by the Communist Government that had been ruling West Bengal for 30 years.

The village panchayats in Nandigram were determined that mosque and temple land should not be taken over by a SEZ — the ominous Social Economic Zones, a three-letter-four-letter word in rural dialect. The West Bengal Government, overconfident because their power had not been challenged in three decades, made reassuring noises promising that not a stone would be overturned without prior notification and permission. Nandigram's villagers were not convinced and the village quickly split into two. On one side were the CPI(M) supporters. On the other the Bhumi Uchhed or Land Dispossessed Group spearheaded by the Trinamul Congress. Supporting the Bhumi Uchhed, but keeping a very low profile, was a group of Maoists who had apparently infiltrated Nandigram from across the Jharkhand border — they were a kind of shadow presence exploding in mines and sniper shots from time to time.

The two sides very quickly came to blows, but the extent of the hostility wasn't revealed till the confrontation with the police on March 14. Nor was the internecine warfare really opened to the media.

It was all the more shocking because the villagers who had confronted the police had apparently gone prepared for an unarmed demonstration. There were women and children in the frontlines of the firing who had apparently been used as shields by their menfolk in an attempt to stop the firing, so while 14 was the official figure of death, it is quite likely that there were many more who went uncounted. Certainly there was a flood of wounded at the nearby hospitals in Sonachura and Tamluk.

The shooting raised an outcry all over the country, with the Governor of West Bengal, Gopalkrishna Gandhi, openly rebuking the West Bengal Government for failing to control the police. Nandigram quickly became the buzzword of the day. Intellectuals all over the city who swore allegiance to the Marxists stood out in protest at the crimes against humanity. The International Film Festival which took place every year was boycotted by filmmakers of the stature of Aparna Sen and Gautam Ghosh — several intellectuals in fact deliberately courted arrest at the main venue of the festival. They were not, they said, opposed to the festival but to the Communist-run Government that had organised the festival, a Government that had forgotten that its role was governing a State impartially without political prejudice. Some of the filmmakers and actors were taken to jail under token arrest but released the next morning.

On the afternoon of November 14, a protest march fanned out across the streets of Calcutta led by the city's most celebrated intellectuals. They claimed that their march was an impartial one designed to condemn police and State brutality. Author Mahasweta Devi spearheaded a drive to gather clothes and medicines for all those people who had left their homes and were herded into camps near Tamluk.

The land went back to the people, the CRPF gradually withdrew. A website, www.14thmarch.com, was set up on the anniversary of the police firing by the artistes of Kolkata who had marched in protest on November 14 and who had then founded a Forum of Artistes, Cultural Activists and Intellectuals. The 'objective' given on the website reads in part: "The West Bengal Government of late has been forcibly acquiring rich arable agricultural green lands in the various parts of the state on the false pretext of industrialisation and development. All of those people who have refused or rejected this heinous scheme of the government, and have been raising their voices against this undemocratic procedure of land acquisition, are being victimised...." The Forum has accused the government of proceeding in a "fascist-like manner to silence all voices of dissent and conducting a shameless campaign of lies". Writer Mahasweta Devi, actor Aparna Sen, theatre director Bratya Basu, academicians Amlan Dutta and Santosh Bhattacharya are amongst its members.

What Nandigram has done is to demonstrate the power that artistic protest can wield. The direct result was Mamata Banerjee's inclusion of singers and artists amongst the ranks of her followers who stood up to be counted in the Local Bodies and Parliament elections of 2008 and 2009. This was followed by a group of intellectuals being inducted into the Railway Ministry — their stated role was to bring a fresh unspoilt perspective and lend a note of culture. She referred to them as her *budhjibi*s.

There has always been a tradition of artistic protest in Bengal and the Naxalite uprising of the 70s involved writers and artists who openly sided with the Left and wrote poems and novels about the cause. However, after the Left came to power they kept their canvases confined to their art. The current set of wise ones hold the flag of activism high, some of them evoking the idealistic glory days of the revolution, organising protest marches and offering to third-umpire meetings between the Centre and today's Naxalites. Because of their efforts candle-lighting has become common in Kolkata.

The question that arises from all this is: what price art? Is it art for art's sake or art for politics sake and is someone going to be active in art's cause? From the *budhijibis'* exploits — and of course Arundhati Roy's — the impression that one gets is art is merely for politics and that the artist exists to be an activist. If that is the case then it is viable enough — Harold Pinter successfully denounced Blair's involvement in Iraq through his political theatre. However, political art demands objectivity from its practitioners for obvious reasons — before choosing a stance the artist should look at it from every perspective and allow all his characters equal freedom to exist.

It may be truthful to say that this is not always the case in India since political activism here has no shades of grey, no perception that a thing can be both true and false. The battle lines are drawn in stark black and white. The system is corrupt and it is time for change. Change how? Change where? Beyond the obvious need to rebel against an oppressive system there are no further directions. Also there is always the underlying suspicion of partisanship and being on one party or the other's payroll.

Bratya Basu's *Bratyajoner Ruddha Sangeet* ('Stifled Songs of the Marginalised') was one of the prime examples of political theatre post-Nandigram and ran to packed houses for a while.

Suvaprasanna, once one of Mamata Banerjee's most

prominent *budhijibi*s, recently exhibited several political paintings, among them a *Last Supper* of a sort painted blood-red with a mummified corpse surrounded by Left Front leaders including Prakash Karat with their left hands significantly chopped off. The comments that followed among the people gathered for the inauguration were not on the brilliance of his art but who-was-who in each painting and what it signified in Bengal's political context. Clearly, a case of politics weakening the impact of art.

More significant art and literature, political or otherwise, appears to be coming from those not directly involved with activism. That makes practical sense — after all, if the intellectual activists are too busy being active or standing for election where will they find the time to create? And there are fallouts. Controversial Bangladeshi writer Taslima Nasreen was one of the earliest of those. After her visa was renewed, a riot broke out in Central Calcutta led by extremist Muslims who declared that their violence was not just about Taslima but also about the Government's inhumanity at Nandigram. The State Government caught on the back foot forced her to leave her home in Calcutta for protective custody in Delhi. Her disappearance occasioned less protest than might be expected.

The Nandigram website is empty now, up for domain grabs — the cause has succeeded, it really isn't necessary any more. Several of the wise ones stood for the April 2011 elections, on both sides of the political banner.

When the questions come round again at a launch this time one may hear something to the effect of: "How do you find time to write in the middle of your busy political schedule? And what are you doing for the good of your constituency?"

෮ఎ

The Story

────

K SATCHIDANANDAN

క౩

It was an ordinary morning.
A handful of jasmines
appeared in a city square.
The next day in another,
and in yet another the following day.

The jasmines whispered to the machineguns
uneasy at their proliferation:

'Revolution no more comes
through the barrel of a gun:
it comes when the taut hearts of
the desperate begin to beat fast
in a single rhythm,
when solitudes of different hues
turn into fluttering flags.

Revolution has shed its habit too
of stealthily arriving at night
along the forest tracks:

now it comes on dancing feet
in the bright daylight:
through a pair of beaming eyes
from inside a veil
looking straight at the sun
from the lightning of the white caps
flung up to the clouds
It comes through the exploding laughter
of the girl riding a tank with her lover
through the thousand-headed song of the future
sung by the single-bodied multitude
without leaders and the lead
through the branching 'V's
embroidered by small hands
on exchanged handkerchiefs.

Revolution spreads faster than viruses
through emails, winks from the Facebook,
flutters its wings from Twitter.
It creates a new lexicon that respells
the gun as cedar, the bullet as orange
and the bomb as rose and finds
new synonyms for man.
It gives poetry a new muscular build
that survives Auschwitz, Siberia and Gujarat.

Treacherous leaders, beware!
Fear our nonviolence!
Jasmines can appear anywhere,
any time lambs can grow eagle's wings
One never knows from which heart to which
this fragrant white current might flow.
It is hard to foretell: like love for us,
and death, for you.

Comrades debating the last laugh,
it is neither the dollar's nor of the bomb's;
It is ours, of fragrant hope ever in bloom.'

(Translated from the Malayalam by the Poet)

ॐ

The Ugly Indian Middle-Class

AAKAR PATEL

ॐ

Twenty years ago, being middle-class in India used to mean "not poor", but it no longer means that.

The middle-class man still does the same sort of thing he used to: he has a job, not involving labour, in the bureaucracy of either government or of a corporation, or he is a small businessman, or a professional. But he is now a consumer of middle-class goods and services as described in the West. This fact, that of his increased consumption and the rise in his numbers, is seen as the remarkable achievement by India in this generation.

Incomes have risen as India's economy has begun merging with that of the world, but what explains the rise in the middle-class's numbers?

This has happened through the expansion of society, by more communities entering the middle-class. This is actually where the big change is being registered, because it is coming about through the inclusion of the peasant castes, the largest social grouping in India, into the urban middle-class.

How is India's middle-class culture being changed and affected by this? Let us have a look at what is happening. First the numbers.

Independent India did not count its population along lines of caste, and it required special surveys, like that of Mandal Commission, to identify the size of peasant groupings. The number was revealed to be over 50 per cent of the population.

The British census before independence told us that the Brahmin population was about 6 per cent, though the community's power and projection in urban India was disproportionate. Three small castes, all put together about 10 per cent of the population, dominated the urban middle classes: Brahmin, Baniya and Kayasth.

What most urban Indians know as middle-class culture is actually the culture of these three communities.

The peasant castes have not had similar access to modernity because they have been away from the city. There are exceptions. Consider the Patel. For over a century he has been travelling and setting up small businesses in Africa and in Europe. His early migration might have been helped by the fact that the Brahmin and Vaishya ban on foreign travel (Gandhi writes about having to do penance on his return from England in 1890) reduced his competition. He absorbed from them the philosophies of being vegetarian and mercantile, but even in America, the Patel retains his peasant self. His business of preference is that of the motel. He secludes himself and his family behind the walls of his property and transacts his business through the cash window. The business does not require him to engage with the American's culture and he is happy with that. His true self unfolds on his visits back to the village in Gujarat, where he builds temples.

If we observe the peasant castes, we notice that there is an absence of high culture because they are not inclined towards it, even when they come into money. Try and make a list of artists, painters and singers you know named Gowda, Reddy, Yadav, Patel or Patil. This aridity will expand as these communities take up more urban and middle-class space.

The second important thing we must consider is the quality and texture of literacy. India was only 5 per cent literate at the turn of the 20th century, and in the last 20 years the direction of urban middle-class literacy is towards English. Increasingly, families speak English even at home and most middle-class Indians do not read in their mother tongue. We are referring here not to the ability to read, which they have picked up at school. They can speak in the mother tongue, if it is peppered with the English words which have become indispensable. We mean regular reading of literature or entertainment in the mother tongue. A very powerful battle was fought and won by Anglophiles like K M Munshi and Nehru against cultural icons like Tagore and Gandhi, who wanted mother tongues to be the medium of education. The arguments on both sides were sound, but the pragmatists won on the evidence of modernity.

This has produced a unique community. There is no parallel to India of a nation whose middle-class is trained to think and approach life in a foreign language, one they have not mastered. India's elite occupy a liminal space, it is emotionally Hindi and intellectually English.

One reason India produces such little literature is that India's middle-class do not own any language properly. Their knowledge of English has come to them through stock phrases because the quality of teaching is poor. Even half-literate Americans speak better, cleaner and more precise English than educated Indians. And on the mother-tongue side, as Tagore and Gandhi feared, the loss of language has resulted in the erosion of India's high culture, its classical inheritance. That is the third thing we must consider, and this can be illustrated.

On April 27 last year, the National Centre for Performing Arts met to discuss a problem: how to get Bombay's citizens to come in and watch their programmes.

The 41-year-old NCPA, set up by the Sir Dorabji Tata Trust, is Bombay's greatest cultural institution. It is home to India's lone ensemble of classical music, the Symphony Orchestra of India. There is nothing else quite like the SOI in India, and there cannot be. This is because the only audience for Classical music in India is here in Bombay. Actually in one corner of the city: South Bombay, the elegant part of the city that the British built and we renamed. And in this part, only in one small ethnic community: the Parsis. About 70 per cent of the SOI's audience is Parsi. The SOI finished its eighth season this year, and every concert was sold out. Tickets in the back rows for some performances cost Rs 750, and sponsors who left their few donor seats unfilled were criticised from the stage.

And so the April 27 meeting wasn't about attendance for classical music. The Parsis, till they are around, and that will not be too long, will nurture European music in India.

The problem is attendance for Indian music and Indian dance. The NCPA, like every other institute in India, has a problem bringing Indians in to listen to Hindustani music and Bharatanatyam.

To address this, the NCPA invited writers on culture to the April meeting, and told them about plans to improve audience numbers. I was one of the half-dozen writers who sat around the table with 10 NCPA officials as its chairman, Khushroo Suntook, told us what his problem was. "We need to build audiences," he said. "As an institution committed to presenting classical and folk performing arts of the highest quality, we can see the red flags being waved with respect to dwindling audience numbers." He brought up a recent article in a newspaper referring to this, and said it had alarmed him. "As an organisation committed to quality, we are doing something about it. We need to make classical and folk art more accessible."

Why don't Indians like to listen to Hindustani music and to watch Indian dance? It's a strange question to ask because Hindustani's great performers are revered. But reverence comes easily to us and the data show that Indians are not particularly interested in their music.

To see the extent to which Indians patronised their culture, I asked a friend to send copies of the magazine *TimeOut* from New York, London and Hong Kong. I compared the cultural events in these to those in Mumbai, Delhi and Bangalore. All six magazines were from more or less the same period. Here's what I found:

In one week (22-28 October), *TimeOut New York* listed 65 classical music concerts, including 15 operas. Of these concerts, eight were free. New Yorkers watched 51 classical and modern dance shows (two free) and attended 86 museum events, of which seven were free. All of this is high culture, corresponding to Hindustani or Carnatic music. Then there were 412 live concerts of popular (including jazz) music, of which 25 were free. New York City has eight million people. After New York I looked at New Delhi.

In two weeks between 16-29 October (*TimeOut* is a fortnightly in India), Delhi had eight classical concerts, including one Western classical performance. Every show was free. That is an average of one classical music performance every two days for a city of 12 million. There was a Spic Macay festival and that was also free. There were 10 shows classified under rock / pop / international but of these only two were free. In two weeks Delhi had six classical dance performances including three Bharatanatyam, one Kathak and one Odissi. All six were free. Incidentally, there were 11 listings for Salsa and Jazz dance classes, none free.

Next, a week in London (15-21 October). Londoners saw 101 classical music concerts (eight free) of which 12 were operas. They saw 45 dance performances of which six were free, and they heard 278 popular music concerts of which 32 were free. London has seven million people.

In two weeks between 16-29 October, Bombaites saw 12 concerts of which nine were free. But the three concerts Bombaites paid to watch included one playing Bollywood songs and a performance by a South African Western classical group. Meanwhile, there were 23 events in pubs and discos, of which seven were free. In 15 days, Bombaites watched two dance performances, including one Bharatanatyam. Bombay has 19 million people. Now let's see Hong Kong, which has seven million people.

In two weeks between 14-27 October, Hong Kong had 14 classical concerts, none free, and the cheapest ticket was $100. There were another five classical concerts listed under 'Events' of which two were free. It had 33 popular music concerts of which nine were free.

In 15 days between 16-29 October, Bangalore had six concerts, three Carnatic, two Western classical and one fusion. All six were free. Bangalore also has seven million people.

Two things become clear, and they're related. One, Indian cities have few cultural events. Two, these are free. Why is this so? Unlike Europeans and Americans and Chinese, we don't pay for culture. So why don't we pay for entertainment? The answer is that we do: we will pay Rs 100 to watch a film, and Rs 200 to enter a pub with a DJ. The reason we do not pay to listen to Hindustani music and watch Hindustani dance is that it isn't entertainment.

The middle-class might revere it, but does not enjoy it enough to pay for it. Our classical culture has withered, as NCPA is discovering, because it is irrelevant. This is a loss because it is one of the world's great art forms. And hundreds of Indians, who know this, have spent their lives in its pursuit.

Let's look at the story of one such individual. Subhashni Giridhar wants to dance for a living. She is a chartered accountant by training, and says she would have given up her profession — and would give it up today — if she could get to perform without having to pay. Not making a living by dancing, mind you, she knows that isn't going to happen. She just does not want to lose as much money as she does now to put her art on display. This is the strange thing about high culture performances in India. The artiste often needs to pay to entertain. The audience does some form of service just by presenting themselves at the performance, and actually they are mostly unattended.

Subhashni began learning Bharatanatyam, at the age of eight, out of love, not the coercion of her parents. We know this because she had to stop dancing to put herself through college, because she had no money to do both, and then picked it up again when she could afford to.

Subhashni became a chartered accountant, and practices with a firm in Bombay. "After I earned some money, I gave my first programme at age 25," says Subhashni. She became a good enough dancer to be asked to showcase the art form by the governments of Tamil Nadu and Maharashtra.

She practices every morning, for two hours, as training for public performances that almost never happen. How many shows does she do in a year? One, and in some years not even that. Of these shows none is ever ticketed. She has been paid for performing, however, and twice by the

NCPA. Once for dancing at the Little Theatre, and the second time at the Godrej Dance Academy. For both these performances, one in 1994 and the other in 2006, Subhashni was paid Rs 5,000. About 60 people attended, she says, many of whom she had asked to come.

She paid the accompanying musicians — vocalist, nattuvanar, violinist, mridangam, flautist — Rs 20,000 for each performance. She says she also must pay for makeup and a fresh costume. If these costs would even out against what she was paid, Subhashni says, she would quit as chartered accountant and perform full-time. She practices in the hope that this will happen.

Dance at the NCPA was managed till recently by Arundhathi Subramaniam. A very elegant woman — tall, slender and quite beautiful — Ms Arundhathi is also a poet. We were introduced at the NCPA lunch, and later I approached her to discuss Subhashni's experience.

I asked about what sort of audience there was for classical dance in Mumbai. "There isn't a real audience," she says. "People have to be wooed and cajoled and conned [sometimes by clever titles or programme notes liberally peppered with words like 'innovative' and 'experimental'] into attending classical dance recitals."

In her year at the NCPA, Arundhathi looked at the problem of paying audiences first hand. "There hasn't been a culture of paying for our classical arts. Even in Chennai, during the December season, people aren't really willing to pay large sums of money for Bharatanatyam."

I asked Arundhathi why it was that when so many girls were sent off to learn dance there were still so few people coming in to attend dance shows. "It's true that good middle-class girls are routinely sent off to learn what's often called 'Indian dance'. The idea on the part of hopeful parents is to turn out accomplished young women — with one more qualification on their bio-datas [probably to improve their marriage prospects, among other things]. But most of the time, neither the teacher, the parent nor the student quite know what's happening. More than one school principal has told me in the past year that their dance teachers have started teaching Bollywood-inspired numbers to their students. So while these masquerade as classical dance, most of these classes are teaching a kind of folk-filmy-*natyam*. And often, a lacklustre kind. Nowhere near as lively — or as cool — as the neighbourhood Salsa or Jazz ballet class, I'm sure."

Of the SOI's 202 patron members, 122 are Parsi. The SOI's musicians are mainly Kazakh, because Indian musicians are not good enough to play in a symphony orchestra. Of the around 100 musicians in the SOI, only 11 are Indian. Of these 11, nine are Catholic. Hindus and Muslims are not interested in listening to this music, and have no skill in playing it. In eight seasons, this hasn't changed.

This fact separates India's middle-class from China's, because Chinese have taken very strongly to classical music in their own country. As the middle-class Indian community expands and may properly be compared with their counterparts in the West, we will be able to examine them even better. But it is disappointing to look at urban Indians today and the behaviour of the educated Indian because it is still primitive.

The opportunism of the Indian does not disappear with his entry into modernity, where trust is higher. Where we can bend the rules towards our end we will do this. We do not have to go far to see this: a society reveals itself in motion and our traffic says all that needs to be said about the low trust in our culture and our opportunism.

We can also observe this on international flights when Indian parents who can walk perfectly well queue up to be carted about on wheelchairs. The reason for this is that the airports in the West intimidate them and they do not wish to negotiate the terminals on their own. The wheelchair attendant is a sort of babysitter for them who takes them through the process without their having to apply themselves.

Do all communities improve in time? Not necessarily. The beautiful drains and gutters of Mohenjo Daro are often cited to show how urban planning in ancient India was advanced before it was in Europe, and it was. However, what isn't as repeated is the fact that many of the drains and gutters had collapsed during the period of the city's occupation and had remained in a state of disuse through centuries before the city was finally abandoned. The people living in those homes with blocked gutters had gone back to their more primitive state. There appears to have been a regression in the Indus community away from modernity.

It is like the mighty highways built by Rome. As Christianity took Europe into the dark ages, medieval Europeans did not how to maintain the high-tech roads built a thousand years ago and let them decline. In both cases, a superior culture was superseded by a lesser, more populous one.

In which direction is modern India moving? Our identification of India is with that of the urban middle-class. We see a new India full of middle-class people who will contribute to the universal civilisation, lifted up through education and through employment. Perhaps this will happen, but the evidence shows the emergence of something quite ugly.

Bullshit as a Cultural Force

MANU JOSEPH

ಲ

The melancholic cow, who crosses the street like an Indian and may transmit good fortune to those who touch her, is probably the most researched animal in the country. In many sprawling places, scientists, who are somewhat infatuated with the sacred beast, are trying to prove that almost everything it does brings benefits to humans. That is why at four every morning in a Nagpur cowshed, volunteers stand with bottles waiting for the cows to pass urine. This is part of an institute's ten-year-long research, worth about Rs 3 crore, which aims to prove that cow's urine can cure cancer, arthritis and renal failure.

Bhanwarlal Kothari, who heads Rajasthan Gau Seva Sangh, a cow fan club, claims that if cowdung is smeared on a wall, it can block nuclear radiation. "We asked Bhabha Atomic Research Centre to test it. We are waiting for them to get back to us." Professor Madan Mohan Bajaj from the Delhi University's department of physics and astrophysics has spent over 15 years investigating the effects of animal slaughter on earthquakes, air crashes and other disasters. "I have noticed that immediately after any festival, when a lot of cows are killed, there is very strong seismic activity around the world."

Evidently, there is a lot of effort that is going on to prove that the great ancient Indians somehow knew that the cow was a very special animal and in their wisdom bestowed upon it an eternal celestial status (as opposed to a Dalit complaint that Brahmins loved the cow simply because it was white, and not the buffalo which was black).

The consecration of the cow, which is not merely a consequence of religion but also Indian nationalism, is the least significant effect of a vastly powerful but underrated and much-maligned cultural force called bullshit. Bullshit is all around us. It is on the hoardings, in the speeches of the most powerful men, the prose of honest women, the analyses of the brightest investment bankers, and even the proverbs of your mother.

Nonsense is a relentless force which is far more influential than sense. It is the indestructible power of nonsense that has ensured that you have read at least once, "Rekha is an enigma" (this actually means she almost never grants interviews to journalists). And it is the same force which is the reason why, despite all the films and serials you have seen, you may find it hard to meet a single person in Bombay who uses the word '*apun*'.

The first spasm of hysteria around India's mythical software power, too, was partly created by this quaint force that was understood so well by the late Dewang Mehta, former head of Nasscom, a pressure group for software companies. He knew that journalists wanted stories and to strengthen their stories they needed figures that they could attribute to an organisation. Nasscom was an organisation, and all Dewang Mehta now needed was statistics. And he always somehow found them. Stunned by the kind of data and numerical estimations Mehta could give out, a friend and I decided to test him by creating a question that could not have an answer. So, on the sidelines of a press conference, we asked him, "In three years' time, by what percentage will the cost of Chinese outsourcing undercut Indian outsourcing?" He answered immediately, in the middle of opening a door, "36 per cent."

A few years ago, at the Ad Asia summit in Jaipur, Kumar Mangalam Birla said in the middle of an India-is-so-great speech that one-third of Nasa is occupied by his countrymen. He was a victim of a type of speechwriters who Google for material. Or, he was yet another recipient of those patriotic chain mails that will eternally crawl through the Internet, listing out the seeming achievements of Indians, almost all of them untrue, like how this many Indians are doctors in America, that many are scientists, and how Sanskrit is the best language for computer coding.

In the middle of all this, if a Sardar somewhere uses a washing machine to make *lassi*, we will point to him and say with flared nostrils of appreciation, *"jugaad"*.

But the most enduring myth is that something called the freedom movement got India freedom, that the Second World War and the impoverishment of Britain had nothing to do with it, that it was just a coincidence that without Gandhi and other sepia barristers Sri Lanka still got its independence in 1948, and soon African colonies too broke free. We would like to believe in the enchanting influence of Gandhigiri as the single absolute force that drove away the whites who probably went muttering, 'bloody Indians', an expression that was enthusiastically attributed to Englishmen by innumerable Hindi films. Interestingly, the American bodyguards of Angelina Jolie and Brad Pitt who tried to control a mob in a Bombay school during the shoot of the film *A Mighty Heart*, have been sued by the slighted mob for calling them, 'bloody Indians'. "*Hum ko* 'bloody Indians' *bola*". Try to imagine the situation. Some American bodyguards, none of whom is named Bob Christo, calling curious Indian onlookers, 'bloody Indians'. Unlikely. But those guards will face charges for insulting the nation if they ever return to India.

Bullshit does not always need the medium of nationalism or other strong emotions to travel far and wide. Sometimes a phrase, an expression which means nothing really, becomes a tradition. Like for instance, after the 26/11 terror attacks in Bombay, when almost every politician including the Prime Minister complimented the city for its "resilience", they did not have to know what they were talking about. They were merely following the political etiquette of calling a city resilient after it has been blasted by terrorists. All over the world, it seems, important people attach no value to the words that come out of their mouth. Because they have a profitable disrespect for a world that is so easy to fool. Just five days before Lehman Brothers went bust, its CEO Richard Fuld actually said, "We are on the right track to put these last two quarters behind us."

A couple of years ago, a public relations firm hired by a young actress seriously considered approaching cricketer Mahendra Singh Dhoni so that a romantic link-up could be manufactured between the two and the news leaked to the media. "They didn't go ahead with the plan for some reason," an executive of another PR firm says. "But this is routine. All those snippets you see in the papers, most of them are total rubbish or half-truths that come from the PRs. We know what the media likes, and we provide it. It is an unspoken mutual arrangement. The only fool is the reader and the chap who watches news channels. Or, maybe even he knows it is all a farce and everybody is just having fun. In fact, even fresh inexperienced actors who hire us ask if they should go to a night club and pick up a fight or do something like that which will get them attention."

Pritish Nandy, journalist-politician and film producer, describes a certain kind of films as, "poop films", whose production budget is vastly exaggerated in the off-the-record interviews given to journalists. "These films are called blockbusters before they are even released. You will hear strange news, like say that an actor jumped off a building during the shoot and nothing happened to him. You will hear that the hero is getting paid so many crores. Then you will hear that the film is a big hit even if the halls are going empty. Then the guys who made the film vanish until they reappear with their next film."

It must not be presumed that the common man is an innocent victim stranded in the middle of all this deceit. In all probability, he is part of the game, he is willing to be had because reality is something like an Assamese film — water boils, lugubrious woman combs her hair, then everybody dies. So the beauty of nonsense is that, in a way, there are no victims. And that is the beauty of Indian film awards, too. It is more entertaining for the general population to accept the farce than question the process.

In an earlier interview, producer Manoj Desai told me, almost casually, about the time when his film *Khuda Gawah* bagged seven Filmfare awards. "It should have won nine. But I could not purchase the other two awards. Someone highly placed in Filmfare told me that Amitabh and Sridevi would get the awards if some pending bills in the Centaur Hotel could be taken care of." After this story was published in *Outlook*, there was no reaction at all. Not a single call, not a single letter from any reader. Nobody cared, or everybody except the reporter knew it already. It was a flop story.

For a particular kind of people who are in the pursuit of intelligence, the most moronic moment in cinema arrived towards the end of a Karan Johar film (which starts with the letter K), when Kajol began to sing the national anthem and people in the audience rose to stand in attention. But Johar is in reality a far more naive master of nonsense than the gentlemen who made what used to be called art films. In the past, actor Naseeruddin Shah has spoken about how some art films were made — "sign me up, borrow funds from NFDC claiming to make realistic cinema, use indoor shots to save money, producer and I split the remaining cash."

There are times, however, when the film industry has claimed it has been wronged by the ethereal forces of nonsense. About four years ago, Ram Gopal Varma had to shelve a film called *Nimmi*, a story about a girl who is lost in a jungle. Powerful animal rights activist Maneka Gandhi, who read the script did not approve of the villain of the film — a tiger. According to a person associated with the production of the film, she told him, "You guys are creative, why don't you write another story." (She denied this episode when I called to verify but she confirmed that she will not tolerate a tiger as villain.) The fear of Maneka Gandhi is so intense in the industry that several period film proposals have been reconsidered because such films are not possible without the use of horses. Shah Rukh Khan still seethes with rage when reminded about how Gandhi had asked him why he used so many pigeons in *Paheli*. With his new visual effects lab and the ability to create animals through software, he says triumphantly, "Now with technology she won't have any problems. We can make animals, beat animals and even eat animals."

The economic might of pure rubbish becomes apparent when we consider that a sizeable portion of the Rs 1,300-crore television news business comes from covering the story a Kuni Lal who predicted the exact time of his own death (TV crews waited outside his house for the moment which passed without his demise), or the stories of scores of people who have had past-life experiences, or a car that travelled in Delhi without a driver (one channel had a panel discussion in which a member discussed the science of invisibility), or the discovery of a giant human face on a Martian mountain (a channel began to claim that life has been discovered and beamed a passionate ticker, '*Kab hoga jung*'), or the endearing tale of one Gajraj who claimed to have met the god of death, Yamraj, due to a clerical error on the part of Yamraj's office. Gajraj even recalled that when the death god realised that the wrong man had been brought to him, he scolded his attendant, "*Ullu ke patthey, yeh kisko uttha laaye ho?*" All this, on primetime national news channels.

Rajdeep Sardesai, editor-in-chief of CNN-IBN, says, "We cannot run away from the fact that today entertainment is a powerful part of our lives, and news has become that. But I am not among the people who say there is no choice. I believe serious journalism matters. The farcical side of television news will eventually die once people see through it."

But the greatest impact of nonsense in modern cultural transaction has come in the form of political correctness. So, Obama is not Black, he is Afro-American; an actress is "an actor"; a prostitute is a sex worker; a housewife is a homemaker; and if you do not believe in global warming, the beautiful liberals have said explicitly, you are an idiot. Do you have the right any more to suspect global warming? Are you allowed to say that global warming is a natural geological phenomenon, that even back in 1912 when the Titanic sank, glaciers were melting faster than they should? Can you say this today and hope to secure the love and respect of any of those beautiful girls in FabIndia *salwar*s?

In some schools in England where gender equality is taken very seriously, the parable of Three Wise Men has transformed into Three Wise Women, and baby Jesus in the crib is a baby girl. Also, today the best desk editors anywhere in the civilised world are under pressure not to use the pronoun 'he' as a neutral reference to God (the devil may be referred to as 'he'). And 'man' cannot be used anymore to refer to humans.

This is a moronic pretense of modernity because, as historian Jacques Barzun has explained in his book, *From Dawn to Decadence: 500 Years of Western Cultural Life*, the word 'man', like many other words, has two meanings. One is male, and the other is human. In fact, the most demeaning word in the English language is 'woman' because, from an etymological point of view, it refers to someone whose existence is defined by a relationship with a man. Also, it is astounding that when there have been so many brilliant women writers who have created remarkable prose about women, the feminist slogan that has stood out is: 'A woman needs a man like a fish needs a bicycle'. Popularised by feminist Gloria Steinem, the slogan not only reeks of a certain literary impoverishment, but is also not factual as evident from the lives of almost all the women we know, including Gloria Steinem who in the year 2000, at the age of 66, to the resounding gasps of impressionable girls, married David Bale, the father of *Batman*, Christian Bale.

Why are there so many things in the world, so many statements, so many concepts that have no meaning at all? How is it that suddenly there are no Indian Mujahideen (IM) terrorists? They are all now, once again, from that vintage Lashkar-e-Toiba. Why is it that sometimes when you read a Booker prize-winning author, you do not see why it is so highly regarded? What is happening in this world? Why is it so easy to fool people? Why is there so much nonsense all around?

Probably because we are not as smart as dogs think we are.

A Yaksha *in* America

THACHOM POYIL RAJEEVAN

ಹ

Yaksha: I am a Yaksha and this lake belongs to me. What is water? Tell me the answer and only after that you can drink the water.
Yudhisthira: Sky is the water.

— The Mahabharata

You may be asleep now.
Not only you,
Our fathers, mothers, children
Brothers, neighbours, enemies
Our dogs, cats, cows
And the dead we imagine
On the stones in the southern yard
All may be asleep.

Our continent our country our language
Our shrines, graveyards
Our bazaars, bathing ghats
Our martyrs' tombs, our parliament
Our ministers, priests, poets,

Our revolutionaries, prophets
All may be in darkness.

Tonight too
You may have forgotten
All that you forget before you go to bed.

There might be leftovers on the table,
Water dripping from the toilet tap,
The fan in the sitting room rotating simply,
A midnight movie playing on the T V for nobody,
The front window open,
By which, your unconsciousness may be saying,
A light or a shadow is passing.

Now, you may be turning to the other side
Chiding me for coming late as usual;
Though asleep, you are careful to keep your gown tidy.

I'm now on the other side of the earth though
I can touch you now
I can close the book that remains open on your bosom
Switch off the song that glides over you.

Continents, mountains, the great oceans,
Strange customs and the unknown languages
Were between us
Only when we were lying close
Touching each other.

At Madison Square
I met a baby squirrel yesterday.
It hasn't heard about our Vedas or the Epics,
It hasn't read the Kamasutra, Arthasastra or the
Natyasastra

It doesn't know Vivekananda, Gandhi, or Jawaharlal
Nehru
But, it knows you
It can understand our language.

Not only it,
The snow in Chicago
The rain in Iowa
The cold wind in Virginia
The trees on the Mississippi
All speak our language.

Now, sleep may have crossed the border of our country
It may be moving the route through which
Alexander, the lame Timur, Vasco de Gama and
Viceroys came;
The Arabian deserts may be half asleep now
Europe may be readying for sleep.

A few moments from now on
When you get rid of morning hangovers
I too will have slept;
But this pain,
From which province of my body or mind it originates,
I don't know,
Will remain awake even then.

ౡ

A Time to Pray...

A J THOMAS

ಐ

By the time these words come out in print, Ajdabiya, my city, could possibly be reduced to rubble, going by the BBC report on the evening of 14 March 2011 — the city is being bombarded from land, sea and air, and there is a threat to kill anyone who resists. The beginnings of these multipronged attacks were reported in the *Hindu* on 11 March.

This is my city, my gentle city, the city I love so much! When I began life here two-and-a-half years ago, teaching English in the local branch of Garyounis University, Benghazi, Libya, I was soon captivated by this haven of culture and tradition. The people are so friendly and warm, never missing out on 'salaaming' you with a smile. They are generally so honest and upright that if you forget to pick up what you bought from a shop and went back there a couple of days later to claim it, the shopkeeper would hand it over to you with a smile. No theft, no violence that we knew of — such a stark contrast to the quotidian Delhi life which I had grown accustomed to over a decade. The largely Mediterranean climate and alluring vistas of sun and sand and greenery mixed up, foregrounded by the cityscape of flat rooftops as I saw it from my fifth floor apartment which I called 'my house in the sky,' had made me gush with poetry then...

Most of our students are from Ajdabiya and Brega, while a few are from Az Zwetina, the coastal town with an oil-terminal barbour, and Sultan, on the Benghazi route. Lying 80 km to the west on Tripoli route, Brega sends us many of our best students. Brega was the scene of terrible fighting lately, with the regime troops and the opposition capturing and recapturing it alternatively over the last several weeks.

Ajdabiya is a metaphor for any other Libyan city such as Misuratha, Az Zawiah, Al Baida, Darna or Tobruk. Though local cultures vary, the essential Libyan character is stamped on everyone. Basically gentle, friendly people, who do not frown, or say 'no' to anything. Even if something impossible is asked of them, they will just say with a smile, 'bukra' (meaning, 'tomorrow'). Outright denial is simply not there in their culture. They are also a very proud, dignified people, who intensely love their country. The greatness of Libya is something even the schoolboy on the street wants you to acknowledge. Now, when there happens to be more than one opinion as to how the affairs of the country should be run, things have taken a grave turn. I can't imagine that any Libyan can be less patriotic than the other. Yet, people die in their thousands for their dissenting voices. I find this strange as a citizen of India, where the Prime Minister and even the President, are open to criticism and comment, and, where, except for a brief interim of 19 months some 35 years ago, freedom to express one's opinion is a given, despite growing signs of intolerance by the state. At any rate, in India we can still speak our minds mostly on anything, at least for now...

When the 'jasmine revolution' erupted first in Tunisia,

and, a month later, in Egypt, the Libyans were found watching the scenes on TVs in shops and restaurants. We thought they were following it like some action movie. No one expected them to be swept off by the wind of freedom that blew over the region. The youth we knew were content with their 'sevens' football, coffee and cigarettes, driving their cars very fast late at night when the roads were empty, braking them abruptly with an eerie screech of rubber on tarmac and wheel-spinning the vehicle like a top — like a buckling rodeo stallion. There had never been gatherings or meetings of any sort that we had witnessed over the last 30 months here, except on very special occasions like the 40th anniversary of the Al Fatah Revolution, the visit of the son of the legendary Omar Mukthar to inaugurate a function etc. There are no cinemas or theatres here where people would gather. The boy students in the university are the exact opposite of their Indian counterparts. They are generally shy and non-assertive in classrooms which are dominated overwhelmingly by girls.

Living standards in Ajdabiya are comparable to any European city or town I have seen. The upkeep and maintenance of streets and homes, the public health and hygiene activities, the transportation used, are all of the First World. Of course, there are less privileged people in the outskirts and the villages, but the availability of five *kubja*s (coarse bread) for *rubah* (one-fourth of a) dinar, and rice and provisions at negligible prices from PDS shops ensured there was no poverty. The per capita income of a Libyan is US $14,884, according to 2010 statistics. Even if one gets only 10 per cent of it percolating down, life cannot be in deprivation. So, reasons for the unrest are simply not financial. As an affluent Benghazi couple who were interviewed by a BBC journalist put it, it is human dignity and freedom that they are fighting for.

Neither are there ideological or religious polarisations.

Obviously Al Queda has no place here. Osama bin Laden's pictures are not displayed anywhere, unlike in some Pakistani cities. Whatever the US military and NATO say about 'flickers' could be about some similar-sounding names that popped up in their investigations. In any case, Robert Gates, the US Defence Secretary, and Lindsay Graham, a leading Republican Senator, have dismissed this reference as insignificant. Libyans are moderate, rightly religious Muslims, though a little orthodox, much like my own people who are orthodox Catholics from Palai! When they exclaim: "Allahooo Akbar! Laa Ilaahaa Illallaah," they are simply submitting themselves before the Almighty, thus strengthening their resolve to take on impossible odds, in His name.

The first mass rally I witnessed was of about a hundred people, waving the green flag of the regime. A few days later, on 16 February, I saw a crowd with no flags marching by, cars and pick-ups lined up in their hundreds, hooting their horns in an unbroken stream of ear-splitting noise… and a few hours later, smoke columns rising to the sky from various parts of the city. Over a dozen government offices and People's Committee offices had been torched. Later I learned that four boys in a procession that had marched towards an army camp had been shot dead. The processions on 17th and 18th grew stronger in number and clamour, following their funerals. By now, the tricolour of the pre-1969 period had begun to be sported by the protesters, passing by mostly in pickups and cars. People who had dreaded even to pronounce the 'G' word, had pulled down the many portraits of Col. Gaddafi exhibited at public places. Walls and smooth surfaces were filled with graffiti that opposed the regime, and called for a new beginning.

On the 19th night, the crowds grew into their thousands. There was great celebration and jubilation. The liberation of the eastern region had been announced. Hundreds of pickups arrived from the outbacks carrying all kinds of people including the elderly and the middle-aged from the various tribes. Fireworks lit up the sky. The rack-a-tack of the celebratory automatic gunfire mingled with the loud explosions of the skyrockets. Women and young girls ululated from the rooftops. It went on until the small hours of the morning reminiscent of a Ramadan night. One scene that I wouldn't forget from that night is that of a grand old man descending from his pickup followed by a middle-aged man and a youth, possibly his son and grandson, and a three-year-old girl-child with a flower-like face, who all danced together amongst the merrymakers!

Soon, the city took over a new character. The hundreds of Bangladeshis, Egyptians and other sub-Saharan people who did the basic cleaning and maintenance work for the Libyans, disappeared en masse. The Libyan youth, hitherto unaccustomed to any physical labour, volunteered to keep the streets clean and the waste-bins emptied, Tahrir-square style. At the junctions where traffic lights didn't work, youngsters controlled the traffic. All the shops were opened. Ajdabiya was normal, literally. As the National Transition Council of Libya was formed, subordinate local committees were formed, (with their representatives in the NTC), in all liberated Libyan cities. Governance had come back to normalcy everywhere, with such committees in full control.

Within a couple of days, there was a total shutdown. I was told that it was a general strike. The gentleman who volunteered to drive us to the bank asked me: "Don't you have strikes in India?" "Yes," I said. "But our strikes are acceptable in a democratic system." He couldn't follow what that was, having grown up in a political vacuum for the last 41 years, but he knew this was their ultimate sign of defiance.

On another occasion, another person who volunteered to drive us said he was a high-ranking officer in the army, and had been jailed for a long period subsequently, for just being 'patriotic' as he put it. He was visibly filled with new vigour at the turn of events. He told us to tell the outside world that Libyans will fight to the last man, to preserve the newly-tasted freedom.

The shop-keepers didn't charge even a single farthing more for anything, although an emergency situation had developed, with many Egyptian and Sudanese shopkeepers moving back to their own countries. I was told that the imams in the mosques had specifically told the people not to hoard or increase prices taking undue advantage of the situation, and they had simply followed orders. There were more positive gestures of generosity all around. The family of an Indian colleague was supplied with loads of grocery items by the people around.

Yet, well-wishers warned. "Beware of going out into the streets. Foreigners are viewed with suspicion. Just take rest, eat and sleep!" Yes, we were foreigners. We had nothing to do with politics on the ground. But, we, as teachers, dealt with the youth of the region. Really nice youngsters. Our concern for them, and our colleagues, was real. What were we to do? I chose to go about in the streets during day and night, to get a first-hand feel of things. Life was normal. Children were playing. People of all kinds were walking about. Even when rumours of aerial attacks and mercenaries advancing floated around, people moved about normally. None were running about or in panic. The sight of young men in pickups wielding automatic weapons, displaying heavy weapons, punctuated the sedate atmosphere. As I was returning to my flat one day, leaving the residence of an Indian colleague at about ten in the night, I came abreast of a vigilante group armed with machetes and sticks. As I passed, someone said, maybe, "doktor" referring to me, and the others let out a soft exclamation… "Wallahi" (by God).

The next few days were filled with rumours fired by some hard facts. There had actually been an aerial bombardment of the arms depot just outside the city. Some sub-Saharan mercenaries had indeed been rounded up. So, whenever automatic fire erupted in the middle of the night, one could not be sure whether it was the signal fire of the night-watch of the local committee, or the mercenaries making a depredation. The deep rumble could be of an aerial attack in the outskirts or of a mere cracker. So, expecting a bomb on one's roof on the top-floor apartment, or a posse bursting into one's apartment with guns ablaze were more of a reality, rather than the highly improbable fiction of a Hollywood flick. Sleep-time was shifted to 7 am to noon.

After about ten days like this, the plan of evacuation by ship from Benghazi was announced. Students and colleagues pleaded with us not to go leaving them behind. But some of those who were keen on our safety agreed that it was better for us to leave.

When we finally set out towards Benghazi 160 km north, everything was calm. Nearing Benghazi we were stopped at a couple of check-points manned by anti-aircraft guns and heavy machine guns. The checking was most cordial and urbane.

Benghazi, the second-largest city of the country, where fierce fighting for several days on end saw thousands dead, is the headquarters of the National Transition Council. There was perfect order in the streets and roads we passed, except burnt-out structures that housed government offices, and anti-regime graffiti that filled the walls. Here, too, I went out to the streets at about 11 in the night, mingling with the procession of the youth celebrating their freedom with drums, loud music and rap and celebratory fire. They had only one message: "The mercenaries are everywhere, killing innocent people!"

Except for the 12-hour-long waiting on the pier occasioned by the confusion the many Indian volunteer groups working apparently at cross-purposes caused, the boarding, on 28th February of the *MV Scotia Prince* and the 33-hour sailing to Alexandria were largely uneventful, although the potential danger until we left Libyan waters kept us with bated breath, as news reached us of the aerial bombardment of an ammunition depot in Ajdabiya and of an explosion at Benghazi, close to the house we stayed overnight, that killed 35 people. On the morning of 3rd March, I was put in the first batch that was airlifted to Delhi. The fortnight of blankness of mind said to be experienced by people in front-lines, had ended, and another of waiting had begun.

For me, after reaching back in Delhi, with a self-deprecatory feeling, like a rat abandoning a doomed ship, this has been the time to pray... to pray for my beloved students and colleagues of Ajdabiya and Brega... for the colleague who had to stay back with his three small girl children and a newborn son, his wife and aged mother... for the little Libyan girls who flit by hanging from their fathers' hands, like butterflies... for the serious-faced little boys clad in fancy uniforms totting toy machine guns.... As grief pulls down my heart, I try to buoy myself up, through the only thing I can do now... just pray... pray that let all these turn out to be mere rumour... let my city continue to glow unscathed in the molten gold of the afterglow over the Saharan sands....

'Ajdabiya' has many meanings in local Arabic — the most important two are: 'a place abundant with fresh water'; and the other, 'a perfect place to die.' The first one follows the fact that Romans built an early settlement here, named 'Corniclanum,' more than 2,000 years ago, because of the availability of pure water on this crossroads of ancient caravan routes from west to east and north to south. The second meaning was coined, following the comment of a contemporary of Ibnu Batuta. This religious figure, who was on his way from Morocco to Mecca on a pilgrimage, suddenly realised that he was about to die due to some strange illness. Of all the places along the route that floated into his mind to settle down to a quiet death, was Ajdabiya. Let's wish that the second meaning will not portent the fate of the people of Ajdabiya.

൧

What's So Funny?

GOURI DANGE

৪০

One of the things that has steadily weakened us and will weaken us further in this millennium is our inability to laugh at ourselves. Why have we as a civilisation become either so pompous or such big cry-babies? Like maladjusted brats we squat in the middle of the road and throw a full-blown tantrum the minute we're faced with the slightest opposition and any home truths that we don't agree with. And like all babies, the issue is always about us and us alone. We are at the centre of the universe and no one better say or do anything that will prove otherwise. So any remark about this leader or that, dead or alive, will cause us to scream, shout, bang our heels, spit, and possibly throw up our dinner. We take everything personally. Except of course the real and true outrages of society like rapes, kidnappings, murders of old defenceless people, felling of trees, corruption… for which we have no time or interest, because somehow it's not about us.

When we want to make a point about how shop names must appear in our very own script (never mind the fact that many of us can't spell and write a sensible sentence in that very script), we'll go red in the face and throw stones. When we're asked to wear helmets on two-wheelers and strap ourselves into our cars, and the administration, like a tired and overstretched mother, gives up and lets us just do what we like.

We also think that other people are complete babies themselves. So when visitors turn up from various parts of the world to explore tie-ups with our country, we assume that they can't see for themselves that our roads and electricity suck. We instantly look around, the idiot-children that we are, for some scapegoat and whirl about pointing at the Press for telling tales and 'spoiling the name' of this lovely city. No amount of explaining will get us to understand (or admit actually) that reality is not defined by words. It is defined by what people see in front of them. And what is in front of the whole world to see, without even a single press report to 'prejudice' them, is huge gaping craters, road-works projects that overshoot their schedule by not weeks and months, but entire calendar years, and power cuts and outages galore.

We sulk and grumble and then lash out at books and films that we don't agree with and which have any whiff of dissent, or counterargument, or a different take on history. And it is highly possible that if just one of us begins to wail about it, a whole lot of other babies nearby will wail even louder and throw even bigger fits, without knowing exactly why they're doing it. People may try to reason with us: "*Array*, but have you read what you're objecting to so strongly?" But we're beyond reason, in full fury, as we sob inconsolably and shriek: "We don't neeeed to reeead it, we knoowwww you're calling us names. Waaaah. We hate you, we hate you, get out, we'll killlll you. Mummmmy telll him, nooooo." And then we may throw some of our toys hard at anyone trying to intervene and insert any kind of reasonability into the situation. And while we're at it, we'll break some street lamps, too. Just for the fun of it. Babies are sometimes easily amused.

We're also deeply into tit-for-tat. So aggressively can we play that game, that sometimes we can cut off our nose to spite our face, rioting, burning and even rampaging in hospitals and ourselves having to be hospitalised if something irritates us enough.

The thing is, we were not like this. Not in living memory. We have regressed in the last 25 years. Obviously some strange emotional accident has happened to us. And from being people with the ability to absorb and deal with a multitude of milieus, live in several centuries at the same time, and to reconcile contradictory viewpoints or truths, we have become exactly like the other countries who we are so critical about, who declare: Do it MY way or no way. And like all babies in a huff, we have no sense of humour whatsoever left, when it comes to our various holy cows.

There are many examples in public and private life of how much more pluralistic we once were. But just a small example will do. Just listen to some of the comic Hindi film songs of yesteryear, and you'll see how much more relaxed we were about history, religion, mythology and all those areas that are now highly inflammable and not to be loose shunted. There's a funny-funny old song which begins: *Sikandar ne Porus sey ki thi ladaai… to mai kya karu?*

The song goes on to list various historical and mythological *jodi*s and face-offs, including one from the *Mahab*…. Oh well, I better not spell it out. Go find it for yourself. It's cute and funny, if you're grown up. If the same lyrics were written today, there would be much wailing and gnashing of teeth and blowing of spit bubbles by different groups of big babies.

I won't put here the actual words of the song, because who knows, someone may have a fit, come and throw toys at me, defecate or hurl their baby-formula on my doorstep.

It's laughable that we want the history and biographies of all our saints and heroes to be written up and taught in such a way that children and other cultures cannot learn about the real-life ups and downs in their lives, the moral and ethical dilemmas that shaped them into the great humans they became, their humble beginnings, or how they were misunderstood or rejected at first. No. Uh-huh. We are now so insecure, that we refuse to see any three-dimensional qualities in the people we revere. We want giant-sized cardboard cut outs as heroes, and you better believe that they were born with haloes, their hands folded in *namaste*, and passed on too with haloes, their hands folded in *namaste*. And anyone who suggests otherwise will get beaten up and tarred. And the clincher: those who we choose to become victims of our righteous wrath in this way will always be very soft targets — elderly academics, researchers, research institutions. People who have nothing but a few files and desks to protect themselves with. What brave warriors we are indeed.

Where has our sense of humour gone? Did we have one? A country gets the leaders it deserves, the saying goes. A country also seems to get the humour and humourists that it deserves. Or to change the focus a little: the state of a country's sense of humour is a good indicator of its maturity. Which is not to say that only subtle and cerebral humour is a sign of coming-of -age. It's more a question of the range of funniness that is available, acceptable and coexists in a country. Where do we Indians stand on this count, then?

The Great Indian Laughter Challenge some years ago on TV broke a long drought of humour on TV. "*Pehchaan kaun?*" people began shouting joyously to each other by way of greeting — the signature line of one of the wildly funny fellows of the show. After very long, we have access to homegrown, regional stand-ups whose material ranges from the absurd, critical, witty, savage, scatological, sexual, to the plain silly, and even the stale but still funny.

Before this, on any given evening, if you were surfing Indian TV channels, all you got was the sitcoms that dish out the usual painfully unfunny fare. The material is so pathetic, that even the producer, director, writer and actors seem to know that this thing won't fly unless backed by hyena laugh tracks. And even worse: that electronically produced tyaau-tyaauu-tyauuuu sound that tries, like some steroid, to pump up the flagging funny factor.

Pu La set the tone in Maharashtra with his celebrated and varied wit. So much so that non-Maharashtrians sometimes wish that someone would translate all of Pu La and make him available to non-Marathi speakers. That's a task that should be undertaken only by the great and the good. Not, for instance, by anyone who has ever written the so-called funny sitcoms for TV. These yell-fests are a really poor example of our wit. They usually rely on large, bumptious women badgering their small, mousey husbands at the top of their voices. Yaawwwn. Pass me the remote quickly.

It's the same thing with Bollywood. The eighties and nineties were full of 'comic' sidetracks that invariably involved fat women in ghastly clothes lisping or talking very loudly. Or there would be some vastly annoying gentleman in false teeth or a funny nose, and perhaps a pair of wretched trousers threatening to fall down. And this gent would, throughout the film, have some signature phrase like *'chunna lagakay'* or some such bilge, that he repeated so many times that you waited for the day that the actor concerned wouldn't pay up the Dubai dons and mercifully for some of us get shot in the head at pointblank range on the Andheri-Versova Link Road, or some such infamous spot. Only Johnny Lever stood out as genuinely funny — possibly because he brought his own material to the film. (And before him Mehmood and a few others, of course.)

In public life, we're constantly whirling this way and that to see who's laughing at any of our holy cows; we squat in the middle of the road and throw a full-blown tantrum the minute we're faced with the slightest lampooning of any of our holy cows. In fact, the perception of most of the rest of the 'global village' is that we Indians take ourselves far too seriously — Indians depicted in cartoons, comics, comedy shows are usually horribly serious/pompous sorts. And no, I don't think this is some big racist slur. It's a perception. Especially about the contemporary Indian. *The Simpsons* had one episode in which the Indian grocery guy gets all huffy because at the beach Homer knocks down his sand castle — which is self-importantly in the shape of an elaborate Taj Mahal. And how is his huffiness depicted? He says: "You have ruined my national monument, you fat American man." Fitting. Stodgy and full of self-importance. That's us.

This, of course, is all in the mass entertainment, news, public arena. Fortunately, in homes and family gatherings in each and every region of the country, we Indians can still put our own spin on life's many absurdities — the understated, sarcastic Puneri wit, the outrageous Nagpur humour, the pretend-innocent Saurashtra fun, the tangential Tamil take, the double-entendre from small-town Punjab, the laconic deadpan stuff from Gujarat and from rural communities all over the state, the ribald stuff that women's gatherings generate… And, fortunately, at this level at least, it doesn't need laugh tracks and no one pickets no one over words, names, references, and hilarious mimicry. No *supari*s, fatwas, bans and *bandh*s are called. In fact, any wet-blanket objector will probably get rewarded by some more cracks and merciless leg-pulling, till he or she finally breaks into guffaws.

Perhaps we can hope for some of that spirit to infiltrate into our public persona.

56, Lane No 70

————————

M P NARAYANA PILLAI

ഇ

Translated from the Malayalam by
SUNIL K POOLANI

56, Lane No 70, is the title of a door in Bulandaar. The door opens into a corridor soaked in darkness. The corridor ends at an iron-grilled window. Beyond the window there is a yellow-coloured compound wall. The wall blocks the light meant for the corridor.

Near the window, the light resembling the sunrays, which pass through an uncut window, harbours at daytime. In that light sits a girl with curly hair and big eyes, stitching children's costumes. When the darkness spreads from the corridor to the window, with the aid of crutches she collects all the shreds of cloths into a bag and disappears into the darkness.

'The heroine of a shadow play', that's what hornbills call her.

The hornbills stay at the thirteenth number room on the second floor.

In the centre of the corridor, on the left side, light could be seen spread across. While aiming at the light the legs would entangle a staircase. Along with it a strong smell of marijuana, rotten jasmines, urine and *sambrani*.

From the roof of the fourth floor hangs a serpentine concrete staircase. Venturing up, the second floor's red bricks could be seen protruding into the steps. Take two steps, and there is the thirteenth number room where the hornbills reside. Thirteen hornbills. Thirteen symbols of thirst.

Foras Road and Grant Road receive a downpour. The hornbills quench their thirst from the rainwater mixed with orange-coloured dust and motor smoke. The cheap illicit brew helps hide the water's dirt, saltiness and oiliness.

With the help of the crutches the heroine of the shadow play starts her sojourn to sell kids' clothes on the streets. By the time she returns her face is sweltered by the blistering sun. Like a sweltered *raat ki rani*.

The hornbills compare her to the flower, *raat ki rani*, the queen of the night; the white-petal flowers on which the autumn's first rain dews throb. On the rain drops the sky reflects.

Around that time, the father, Ramdhani, who introduces himself 'Gwala', could be seen sleeping below the stairs on a yellow towel printed 'Ram, Ram'. He reached Bombay from a rustic Bihar village with two oxen. A milkman. But he ceased to be a milkman for many years. He was a watchman at Gijibhai's mill. One day, tangling his uniform on the mill's gate, he walked down to Bulandaar in his underwear. What then left were poverty and the name Gwala. The wife fell down at the entrance of Arthur Road

Hospital, and breathed her last. The last spring cleansed by cholera.

Against 56, Lane No 70, there is a lamppost. Also a red signpost that claims the thirteenth number bus will halt there. The thirteenth number bus starts from the seashore where eagles feast on the naked, dead Parsis. The destination is an electric crematorium.

'The survival act of the survival', that's what the poet hornbill termed the movement of traffic on Lane No 70. 'Survival of the fittest.' Recalling the chariot race that apparently happened in Rome. The race is not based on speed, but strength. Colliding on each other and collapsing, the vehicles pace ahead. The weapon of the thirteenth number bus is the First World War's 'smoke-screen'. An immaculate life-and-death moment of the vehicles on the street. The thirteenth number fills the sky with black effluents. Seconds later, once the screen of smoke recedes, all the vehicles will be on the streets.

Where is the thirteenth number?

The hornbills start their journey in the first trip of the thirteenth number towards the crematorium. The dawn might have descended by then. The soot-stained trousers and shirts of the machines. When they return at ten in the night the soot would be decorating their faces and bodies. In one corner of the room, in the sodden light of the kerosene lamp, they take bath from the water filled in the earthen pots. Then the carbolic smell of the cheap, red soap would fill the room. And they go to sleep pressing their faces into oil-stained pillows.

Around that time, in the light of the candle erected on a trunk-box, on an ink-spreading paper with the help of a violet pencil, the poet-hornbill could be seen scribbling something.

C. Vasu is the ever-pristine poetic hub of the poet-hornbill.

If the trunk-box is removed one could see, on the cement floor, scribbled by an iron rod, the name of C. Vasu.

Years ago, in the monsoon season, the poet, who was finding solace in the veranda of a shop, was brought into this room by C. Vasu, and gave him place to lie down.

C. Vasu was a welder who earned twenty rupees a day. Died due to a cough called tuberculosis. The poet had to borrow the thirty rupees meant for the electric crematorium. C. Vasu couldn't repay that debt in the form of currency. That's how this room came into the hands of the poet.

The personal properties of the hornbills are thirteen iron-boxes, thirteen pillows and thirteen earthen pots. And the public properties are the kerosene lamp and the thirty rupees.

The poet is the caretaker of the thirty rupees. Even if hunger threatens to kill him he refuses to touch that money. It is meant for the needs after death. The charge that is to be paid at the electric crematorium. Things shouldn't fail to happen without those thirty rupees.

Ramdhani's snoring and the chariot race on the road outside would continue to break the night's tranquillity.

Apart from the flower called *raat ki rani*, Ramdhani has seven offspring. When five of them reached the age that made them capable to prey, they were scurried away. The remaining two get beaten up by a bamboo stick, and driven away, every dawn. But once dusk falls, they seek the same abode. Two dry wheat *roti*s each would be kept for them.

One day they wouldn't come. That day the practice could be stopped.

The city is the world of the banished people from the country. Hunger banished them. They live on in the faded dreams of a lost spring.

The hornbills on the ornamental, twisted coconut leaves

that adorn religious functions, and the oil-soaked, untied hair; Ramdhani on the *baang* mixed in *badam sharbat*, and the Bhojupri songs, which praise Lord Ram, and are sung in the shade of a lone mango tree in the centre of wheat fields.

The handful of flowers that Ramdhani brings every evening to 56, Lane No 70, is what announces the spring in this desert-like city. There is a picture of Lord Ram in the darkness that surrounds the area beneath the staircase. A picture that shows a hunting scene along with wife Seeta and brother Lakshman. The flowers are meant to be put up there.

The only person who celebrates Holi at 56, Lane No 70 is Ramdhani. He bustles in and out of all the rooms with a paper packet that contains saffron. Sometimes he goes down the streets and sings a couple of ribald songs. And returns in the noon and would take some *baang*. And dream of Lord Ram.

The year he drove away his last son. The hornbill with a long beak and firewood on his head stopped Ramdhani who was venturing into the thirteenth number room with saffron. There is somebody sprawled on the floor. Red eyes. A kerchief tied around the neck.

The face has started sprouting boils.

The same morning he was taken to Arthur Road Hospital.

A sore called small pox.

All of a sudden a silence overwhelmed 56, Lane No 70.

The hornbills were reduced to twelve. In three-four days, the hornbills' number came down further.

One morning, one of Ramdhani's driven-away sons was seen lying down the lamppost, with boils. A few minutes later, a municipal vehicle came and took away the body.

The fifteen-year-old *raat ki rani* clamped on to her crutches and wept.

The poet said the return has begun.

The same day the eighth hornbill too headed towards Arthur Road.

The last news of the first hornbill who had gone to the hospital arrived that day. He wouldn't require the thirty rupees, the common property. That expense will be borne by the hospital. On that day's mail there arrived a letter for him, bearing a pencil-written address. The five hornbills opened it. He has got a son.

Suddenly, the poet ran his fingers over his face.

No problem. They are pimples.

The rest of them looked at each other with suspicion.

One of them sold his wedding ring and drank that night. Drank till surpassing the knowledge that he was alive.

The trust is being lost, the poet said.

The poet was ready to spend the common property of thirty rupees, the charge meant for the electric crematorium. The poet went to the slums where Dravidian stonecutters from Salem live, and brought back marijuana. He sent Ramdhani to get some *baang*. Some hornbills went and beaked their way back with illicit brew. Vinegar, spirit, ammonium sulphate, aspro, tranquillisers, potassium cyanide… like sparrows bringing the twigs to build their nest, they collected all this by evening.

Ramdhani brought saffron, to celebrate a new Holi. In the menstrual blood where beliefs were shattered.

When saffron was smeared the contempt towards pimples receded.

Alcohol made the small pox look like malaria, jaundice, warts or pimples.

When the *baang* that looked like leaf-ground chutney went inside his abdomen Ramdhani became an animal and stood on four legs. The hornbills forcibly opened his mouth and poured into it arrack from a tumbler. Then he became a snake that has had its prey and lain down calmly. The hornbills took him and laid him on the terrace. Like Garuda placing the rattlesnake on the branch of the tree.

Alcohol helped the poet to talk more and more. Four hornbills listened to him carefully.

The poet had indeed loved the *raat ki rani*. Not anymore.

When they heard that, the four went down. They caught hold of the heroine in the shadow drama who was stitching near the window. She tried to wriggle out. Kicked them with her helpless legs. She was drawn up the staircase. Two crutches were seen abandoned on the staircase.

The poet could decipher one more thing. C. Vasu has ceased to become the poetic hub. And C. Vasu is not something that he loathes or loves.

And the poet noted that beliefs and relationships depend on the flow.

Still they ran their fingers over their faces. Seeking a pimple called small pox.

(First appeared in the Malayalam in Janayugam Onam Special, *1964)*

Democracy as Bondage

FARZANA VERSEY

ॐ

If you are Indian, then you are born with fake freedom thrust down your throat. It is this that we regurgitate on special occasions on tricoloured pasta strips, brandishing flags to applaud pampered sportspersons and crying ourselves hoarse at rallies that we descend at holding candles that melt faster than our hardened resolve to make it to prime-time activism.

If you are Indian today, then by default you have a silver spoon in your mouth because you are part of the global economy that shamelessly imports nuclear energy ostensibly to light up villages when villages have been bulldozed to make way for things like the people's car and people's industries.

We are trapped in the 'Secular Republic' business, and business it is for those running the pantomime show. After every performance there is ovation even if the stains show up because we are told, as opposed to our neighbour that, "At least you can choose." What choices do we have?

One year, during Independence Day, I happened to be

in Pakistan. There were people praising Indian democracy. Nice people in nice homes were telling me how fortunate I was. I simulated elation. I have never felt so different, yet so Indian. Pakistanis have had to deal with military dictators and are therefore understandably enamoured of the ability of Indians to throw out governments every five years.

What no one bothers to look into is that for those five years democracy lets people decide and agree upon certain freedoms autocratically designed for them. The idealism of the leaders is in fact a game plan to maintain the status quo. Democracy does not do away with hierarchy; it adds several layers to it. Almost 64 years after Independence, we are still trying to find our feet. There are three factors that cause the most confusion.

Secularism: It started way before 1947, which is the reason we continue to fight over the leftover manifestos of Partition. Mohammad Ali Jinnah's secularism could not translate naturally into democracy for the very idea of creating a ghetto nation is anti-democracy. Pakistan was created for Muslims and secularism was meant to be the icing on the cake. India did not have that option; it was busy dividing the pie. Secularism and religion are not at odds with each other. If we call India a secular nation, then we have several religions screaming out from different directions. We confuse multiculturalism for secularism. Incidentally, religion and parochialism have played an equally damaging role in India despite this rainbow nationhood or, perhaps, because of it.

Modern monarchies: Dynastic politics in contemporary times is an insult to the democratic idea. We often justify it with an, "Oh, we are an emotional people and get attached to these families." Indeed. We are the ones who torture and kill our own, sometimes even before they are born. Our subcontinent is a sad case of slavery passing off as human bonding.

Asif Ali Zardari, when he took over from his assassinated wife, said he wanted to be like Sonia Gandhi. This initially meant pulling the strings and slowly coming into the limelight as a shadow figure. Sonia Gandhi forced Rahul into the fray to save her position and act as her frontman and although now in his forties he is still ambling across the grassroots terrain.

Speaking about Bilawal Bhutto, Imran Khan had said then: "You can inherit a house, jewellery… but how can you inherit other people's wishes, dreams? A democratic political party, being inherited — it is mockery of democracy." It was amusing that he wanted Benazir's son to be like the son of India and it would be wonderful if he "gets educated, and is starting from below — like Rahul Gandhi in India".

While he seemed to have a legitimate problem with home-grown inheritance, he was using the same legacy in India as an inspiration. Apparently democracy, even in name, is a good pennant to hang on to.

TINA – There Is No Alternative: Why? Because no second-rung leadership is created; no one is given an opportunity. People of stature holding important portfolios look like minions in the boudoirs of the ones born with the country in their mouths. But TINA is a coquettish concept. Strangely, it promotes fidelity even as it is poised for a pole dance. It is a riveting sight and prevents the citizens, bonded with herd instinct, from looking elsewhere.

There will be several little people doing big things, but come floods and poverty photo-ops and it will be the sons of the 'spoils' who will be promoted, returning home from exile or slumming it in Dalit shanties. Look, we say, this is what we need. No, this is what we get. Some call it democracy when it really is "manufactured consent".

Democratic delusions must appear real. We are being had. A bunch of leaders decides how we should pay obeisance to the nation. Political groups assume extra-constitutional powers by being 'servants of the people' empowering themselves with a remote control to make the state cower before their diktats. A big fat line demarcates their freedom and ours.

What are the freedoms we are talking about?

Freedom of expression: Have you encountered any aspect of freedom that has not stepped on someone's toes? The national anthem, national heroes, national holy cows, national sports all become prime property, but only when they are in eyeball-grabbing mode. Otherwise, they lie unclaimed in moratoria. Ridiculous-painted faces in country colours provide a seal of approval even as T-shirts bellow, "I love New York".

Some years ago an industrialist Member of Parliament, Navin Jindal, fought and won a case for a licence to fly the national flag at his house. What do such gestures achieve? Do we see the irony of a pampered person flaunting national fealty while he sits in his feudal seat and audaciously takes up the cause of the khap panchayats that pronounce no marriage within the same sub-sect that resulted in honour killings?

Freedom of human dignity: Self-rule was built on the bodies of those who remain nameless. Mahatma Gandhi did not die in a stampede. He was killed not because he fought the British, but because he aligned himself with the Khilafat Movement.

This idea has been sanctified as 'tolerance' in India today, which is by far the worst aspect of democracy. It reeks of patronage of one common man by another, brainwashed into a destructive thought process that grants an entry permit into the mainstream.

The ethnic Swadeshi Movement was essentially a phony idea trumped up to look labour class. It is a slap on our precious democratic faces that khadi is now designer clothing and even Indian government outlets have raised taxes on it, making it unaffordable.

Nehruvian socialism was yapping away at the Soviet model and merely gave more teeth to the government. This was organisation of power, not social idealism. The poor did not benefit from nationalisation of industry. The Licence Raj merely gave the rich incentives to grease the pockets of political parties.

Today, how does national self-esteem fit into the global initiative when we are dumped with Western waste? Why are we still on outdated British laws and religious edicts?

Freedom to be or not to be a nationalist: Patriotic jingoism is antithetical to the idea of democracy for it does not allow exposure of the rot within. Double standards make it mandatory, however, to cheer those who rip their own country apart but only as legitimised media warriors. Societies whose unique selling proposition (USP) is poverty and go to the West with a begging bowl get self-righteous if, along with some coins, the *mastah*s throw in a few homilies because we quake at the country's reputation being at stake. Nationalism becomes an obsessive compulsive disorder as we start on Operation Scrub-scrub from sanitised pedestals.

Terrorism, too, has a decided-upon colour based on a dictatorial concept. We conveniently want to be a cohesive whole when we are fighting amongst ourselves and overriding the rights of others. Our regionalism is no different from the principalities of the pre-Partition era. Democracy is scrawled on the flaky parchment of the past. The goal of history, Tagore believed, is not "the fierce self-idolatry of nation worship". Nationalism is about conformity. It cannot survive if it provides choices, for in doing so it will threaten its own credibility.

A patriot is often co-opted and therefore the enemy of a truly free state of being.

A City Called Madras

TISHANI DOSHI

ಕ

I was born in a city called Madras in 1975. In those days it was a beautiful city; quiet, romantic, with a real port city's easy-breezy feel. Mothers pushed their prams along tree-lined streets, children rode their bicycles without supervision, shops were family-run enterprises, the sea was only ever fifteen minutes away, and nobody minded their own business. Neighbours had names and faces and habits. The roads and rivers, which ran through the city, were lazy and moved with no great sense of urgency. The poor were still poor, but the rich behaved with modesty and caution, stashing their wealth away so no one could cast an evil eye on them. It would appear to an outsider that this was a city of equitable values; that its inhabitants cared about their streets and buildings, and more importantly, about beauty.

You learn a city by its streets and buildings, its trees and neighbourhoods. You remember a city by the footprints you make: daily commutes, shortcuts to favourite haunts, the many journeys out and the journeys back in. I left the city of my birth in 1993. While I was away I dreamed about it as if it were a person from my family, a beloved. As I dreamed, they changed the name of the city. Just like that. The great overthrow of colonialism. It was as if the new city had been lying underneath the old one all along, waiting to assume its shape. Everyone expected the city to be the same, but the citizens of Madras were one group of people and the citizens of Chennai were another. I don't know if the city changed because of its new name, or whether it was I who had changed. Either way, the leaving and the change are tied together.

To live in the city of your birth, abandon it, and then return to it, is to be forever tied to it. It is a relationship that is necessarily dominated by nostalgia. You do not have the freedom of the migrant, the transient, the person from elsewhere, who makes his associations without any reference to childhood. Madras for me is always a place of the past, sometimes a place of the future, rarely a place of the present. The longer I stay in the city, the more memories I accumulate, the less the city reveals itself to me.

To speak of a new city you have to remember the city as it was before. When I think of Madras I think of mathematicians and musicians; curd-rice eaters and coconut-oil users; Rukmini Devi Arundale and J Krishnamurti; Theosophists and Nobel Prize winning physicists; Mahaballipuram, Marina Beach and Moore Market; The Campa Cola Factory and Drive-in-Woodlands; moustachioed men and Mylapore mamis; MGR and Rajnikanth. When I think of Chennai I think of IT corridors, car manufacturers (the "new Detroit"), Kollywood, the Mecca of medical tourism. What's in a name? Madras-Chennai is both those cities: romantic and industrious.

There are a few things that tie Madras and Chennai together, but the main thing is language. Tamil is the oldest living language in the world, and Tamilians are fiercely proud of their mother tongue. Today the language of the poet Thiruvalluvar coexists with the language of auto drivers and college graduates who work at BPOs. The outsider would do well to learn about the ubiquitous "machaa" (something akin to "yaar"), and "palli-pessam," (literally, lizard talk — the ultimate sound of approval, which sounds an awful lot like disapproval). Musician friends of mine, trained in the Hindustani tradition, tell of their first encounter with this Tamilian lizard-like click clicking of the tongue. During a performance at the Music Academy in 1986, every time they started with the kharaj, the entire audience erupted in *palli-pessam*. Startled, the poor musicians tried to tone it down. It was only midway through the show did they realise the tongue-clicking was the Madrasi way of saying "vah vah." Now, they say, they are used to it.

Let it be said: the Madras audience is a most knowledgeable one when it comes to classical music. In the month of December the city is host to the largest music festival in the world. Hundreds of performances take place in *sabha*s all over the city. This is our great claim to fame. Well, one of them. We also have the second longest unbroken coastline in the world, and the second-largest living banyan tree in the world. We also treat our chess players like rock stars. For these reasons and others, it's an immensely original city.

But it's a city that's changing rapidly. The roads are no longer lazy, the rivers cannot move. Big has replaced small. Shopping malls, multiplexes and gigantic apartment buildings are taking over the cityscape. The rich have traded in their superstitions for BMWs, the poor are probably poorer, and beauty is sometimes nowhere to be found. Every once in a while, there are flashes of that easy-breezy old city; a resident who has lived here long might come across a scene and think, *Yes, there is my youth, I see it,* and then it's gone, in a whiff of exhaust fumes.

But let me try to keep nostalgia at arm's length. Let me not be too disdainful about change. It's easy, after all, to criticise pollution and noise and greed. Let me tell you instead about the essence of the city as I see it. Every evening I walk in the Theosophical Society — one of the last green oases in the city. There's a small path that leads out to a stretch of beach, and sometimes I sit with a fellow Madras-friend — wildlife filmmaker, Shekar Dattatri. We wonder at the gift of this beach amidst all the things we're disdainful about. Magical smog-filled sunsets and migrating birds. "What will happen?" I ask, "When the proposed Elevated Expressway is complete, cutting through this space with cars whizzing above our heads?" "We'll adjust," Shekar says simply, looking to the horizon.

One day in the not too distant future, there's a possibility that this city I call Madras and most call Chennai will grow so much it will become a megacity including Pondicherry and all the towns in between. Will they change the name of the city again? Perhaps. One thing is for sure. Its residents will have their eyes fixed to the horizon, because the horizon is the way out and the way back in.

Birth of the Kamasutra

MEENA KANDASAMY

ఙ

A bull in bed himself, Nandy never spoke
Of having seen their non-stop sex.
He signed a book deal instead.

Blushing like Brangelina at its launch
Shivshakti sang this papparazzi's praise.
Goddywood queued up for copies.

Reading between lines sheets shoots, and
Realising they were only doing the done
The gods went into manic depression.

ఙ

Human and Machine

MALINI CHIB

෨

Donna Haraway's essay *A Cyborg Manifesto* (1991) is about how in the twenty-first century technology is embedded in our lives. Haraway argues that human beings are interdependent for technological and human support. Her article mainly focuses on 'white western women' who have access to all technological equipment. Let me describe the various helpers and equipment that I needed to lead a full life, like a nondisabled person. Let me examine Haraway's concept of women in what she terms 'integrated circuit' in relation to my context and how my technological equipment constructs me differently as a woman with a disability.

Haraway argues that a cyborg is a 'cybernetic organism, a hybrid of machine and organism'. Due to my physical disability I needed a mixture of technological aids and people to aid me in my daily life. Human help is vital for anybody who has a disability and I have been extremely fortunate in having excellent help, encouragement and support from my mother, family, paid helpers and friends.

As a thirty-five-year old woman with disability, I need both people and machines to assist me in my day-to-day life. Haraway points out that this technological dependence is very much a western influence. I agree with Haraway to some extent that if I had not had the western influence in my life, I would not be able to afford the excellent technological equipment I have; I would not also be able to function in a world primarily designed for able-bodied people.

Personal Care: Humans as Aides

Till the age of twenty-two, my mother and all members helped me with my daily living needs. My grandmother and my aunts also helped me with my daily living needs whenever they came to spend time with us. This is a cultural difference between the east and the west. The east has the family as a social structure for support in a strong way.

Early days show that the family rallied around. My mother was my primary carer. When I was nine, my mother and Pam took care of my personal needs. I loved this. I was emotionally not ready to have an outside person to help me with my personal care, although we were in India where paid domestic help is readily available. Being professionals, my mother and Pam took care to train me to be as independent as possible. A lay attendant would not be able to have done this as effectively as professionals.

It was only in Oxford that we decided to have my own personal attendant to look after my personal needs. During a visit to Berkeley in the US I found disabled people in electric wheelchairs everywhere. I visited the Centre for Independent Living and The World Institute for Disability. At the Centre the aspect that intrigued me the most was that disabled people live independently with their personal attendants. There is a difference between having a family member or a close friend assisting you with your daily living skills and paying a person to help you. I strongly believe that with a family member or a close friend you have too much of an emotional linkage. A neutral person, as I observed in Berkeley is much more desirable. I decided to get someone to help me.

In America the word 'carers' are replaced by 'personal attendants'. According to Mason the word *carer* has no place in the social model, as the word implies some sort of emotional relationship. I feel the phrase *personal attendants* is far better. I agree with Mason who feels that attendants are people who care about our practical needs and not our emotional needs which our friends and family are supposed to give and not the people who give us help practically.

The medical model stresses that disabled person should be as independent as possible. It sees disability as a personal tragedy. Having a personal attendant is more in keeping with the social model, allowing us to contribute independently in some form. Having to do everything physically tires me out as I do not have any energy to do anything else for the rest of the day. For me to contribute to society and feel a part of society is more important.

Today in the postmodern era the disability movement has moved away to a more rights approach model. In the rights approach disabled people see themselves as essentially having a disabled identity. Their disability is not made invisible. A well-known disabled feminist, Jenny Morris, argues that she is essentially different from other nondisabled women. In her book *Pride against Prejudice* (1991) she feels that women with disabilities should celebrate their differences rather than strive to be like the norm. I agree with Morris as I feel that if I am to be allowed to contribute positively to society I have to acknowledge the fact that I am a woman who is disabled. I require help in certain ways. I think hiring help for personal care is essential. It's a well-known fact that parents of disabled children get burnt out quicker then parents of nondisabled children. For twenty-two years of my life I accepted my mother and my family to help with my physical needs — then I moved on.

I think the concept of hiring someone to help disabled people is more attuned with what Leonard and Delphy feel in *Familiar Exploitation* (1992) that women's work at home is unpaid and unrecognised. Having someone who I employed recognised the fact that 'helping me was a recognised job'.

In Oxford, Maya, a Nepalese woman, accompanied me and was employed as my maid, to assist with my daily living functions. Maya was told that I was the employer and she was to take direction from me. Having a paid person was appealed to me greatly as it gave me more independence and flexibility from my family. However, having Maya around had its good and bad points. My friends would spend more time talking to her instead of me. I noticed that they would feel sorry for her. Attendants of disabled people get automatic sympathy.

My relationship between Maya and me were more of friends than an employee-employer relationship. I was able to have the comfort and support of what I was used to in India, but it made me totally dependent in other people's eyes on Maya. Most people preferred her to be there whenever they took me out.

The downside of having a full-time attendant is that it isolated me from the rest of the community and it did not give me a chance to interact with others. It prevented them from helping me. This impeded my socialisation within the University.

When I came back in 1996 to London, rather than having a full-time attendant from India, my parents and I investigated the personal care system. I only needed an attendant for one hour in the morning and one hour in the evening. This turned out to be most successful. I now have an attendant in the morning and one who comes in the evening.

This I like, as I am independent for the entire day and yet someone coming in the morning and in the evening gives me the help I require. I think the feeling of being alone even for a short period of time during the day was terrific. I can do anything I want. I did not have to explain to anyone. It also made me very organised about my needs. I began to do all my shopping, laundry. Again living in a university set-up where facilities like the canteen, toilets, computers, library facilities all accessible helped greatly.

To mention the problems I encountered in the five years were that there have been times when some mornings or evenings the carer has not come and there has not been a replacement. I had to depend on either my mother or Sathi or, even worse, I had to depend on one of my friends who were sharing my flat at the time to help me. I feel this is not fair on them as they have their own jobs to hold down and helping me is an extra task, which is uncalled for. Clearly a backup system is essential. Without a backup system, I could be stuck alone waiting for someone to come and give me some assistance. Again, waiting on the first floor of a hall of residence (where I live at present) unable to get out even if there was a fire, is a high-risk situation. As Brisenden argues, "Its ruins relationships between people in thwarted opportunities on both sides of the caring equation."

The ideal setup would be if the carer could be more reliable and responsible, if the University's Halls of Residence addressed the personal needs of a disabled student and had a personal support system set up for people with disability.

Technology as Aides

Mason said: "Technology and development are not in themselves all bad. Indeed, disabled people are probably the best example of being empowered by technical means- speech synthesisers, powered chairs, Braille-converting software, user-operated environmental systems all have transformed our lives."

Two of the most useful and necessary technological aids for me that have revolutionised my life are the wheelchair and the computer. With both of them I do not feel as excluded as I would without them.

Mobility

When I was thirteen my parents took my brother and me to England for a summer holiday. I remember I hated the thought of being in a wheelchair. At that time I did not want to acknowledge that anything was different about me. I firmly believed that I would walk independently one day. However, I had to accept that I would probably never walk independently. I would need a wheelchair. At the Thomas Delarue School, which had vast long corridors, I needed an electric wheelchair to move around. I soon found I loved to cover ground and space fast… it was like driving a fast car. During college days too at Xaviers, I used my electric wheelchair extensively. I use to love whizzing around the ground floor in and out of the canteen and the quadrangles. The feeling was exhilarating. For the first time in my life I could move in space very fast without any effort.

I felt like a normal human being.

Communication

Anne McDonald, who like me has cerebral palsy with a speech impediment similar to mine, says in her web-page: "Communication falls into the same category as food, drink and shelter — it is essential for life, and without it life becomes worthless."

Due to my poor hand function I cannot write. At the Centre for Special Education, India, I first used a typewriter. I began typing with one finger. I used to enjoy writing letters and short essays. Leslie Gardner brought the Cannon Communicator in one of his visits to India. Sometime using the Cannon was laborious; I found it cumbersome. It needed a great deal of effort. It also attracted too much attention. I preferred having an interpreter as it speeded things up. But that had its problems. My speech is bad. Therefore, my family and close friends would interpret freely and used to finish words and sentences for me. This was a practice that began with my teachers as well in all the schools. This caused many gaps in my learning process. I rarely used an independent mode of communication, and tended to rely on my family and close friends to interpret my speech!

It was in Delarue that I began to express myself more. For my written work I used an electric typewriter. It was in Xavier's I became acutely conscious of my speech. For notes in class I used to give a carbon paper to one of my fellow students and they would take down the notes and give me a copy. In Xavier's I did two exams, the HSC and the BA.

All questions required lengthy answers within a certain time frame. For the regular student the time given was three hours. For us, the University authorities made a concession and gave us double time which made it a six-hour-long exam! I could not have typed, as my typing speed with one finger was infinitely slow. For both of the exams I needed amanuensis or writers. In the six hours, we had to answer the four narrative essay type-answers, each fifteen hundred words. I had three writers. My speech being poor my writers needed to know the gist of what I was saying, so they had to understand the difficult words in Ancient Indian History,

Literature etc. My writers patiently listened to my dysarthric speech while I spelt out each letter, assiduously. The Canon would be always there, in case they did not understand the odd word. The worst thing was that the exam took place in the heat of May. May is the height of summer in India being 44 degrees. My throat got so dry calling out long essay type of answers that I thought I would faint; I could not speak without sips of water. The whole process was exhausting for both the writer and me. Both of us were ready to get on to stretchers at the end of each exam. Again I passed this time with a Second Class. At Oxford the system of assessment were assignments and examination. The examinations were only four hours long. I got a B+.

The Voice Synthesiser

In 1993, I returned to London. It was as this point my parents and I seriously thought of a more effective communication tool rather than the Cannon. A friend of ours, Professor Klaus Wedell, invited me and my mother to a communications seminar workshop at the Institute of Education, University of London. We went to the Roehampton Hospital in Putney, for an assessment of my communications difficulties. Initially, I was against the idea of having a big communication device like the one Prof Stephen Hawking has, as it was extremely visible and it made my disability look prominent. I was recommended the Toby Churchill Lightwriter. It was small and compact. What I liked most was that I could carry it in my handbag. The Lightwriter is a voice synthesiser, a smaller version of what is used by Hawking. Unfortunately, it has a male and an American voice.

Once I got the Lightwriter I ventured out on my own and found that I made friends very quickly. Times had changed. I found people wanted to get to know me as well and to have an independent relationship with me. It was as if people wanted to hear my voice and learn about my thoughts. The Lightwriter helped me to become more assertive. I began to communicate more, using it. With the Lightwriter I felt I began to think. I no longer could take refuge in silence or garbled responses, and needed to make meaningful responses. Whatever I wanted to say I could easily write. Unlike the Cannon where it was difficult to press the letters, the Lightwriter was easier. Also the letters were placed like a computer keyboard. Thus, it was easier to speak in sentences quickly.

Looking back I was fortunate in having a means of communication strategies setup from a very young age and fortunate that with the variety of inputs from western technology despite serious communication difficulty, I do not feel I cannot communicate.

ॐ

Silence

PRITI AISOLA

౭౦

Poem 1

'Your silence ... swathes of sheer fabric'

Your silence
swathes of sheer fabric
floating in space
wind-wafted
sun-spangled

My words
earth-hitched
of all wanderings forgetful
pitch their tent
for good

Poem 2

'Iron sheets of silence'

Iron sheets of silence piled high
My rain words patter
slide off
Etch no impress

Poem 3

'Your silence … a flute recital'

Your silence
a flute recital
My words
a railway station's
buzz and clang
Yours the kutcheri
Yours the audience
Yours the applause
Encore

Poem 4

'The hem of your silence'

My words strain to touch
the hem of your silence
No greater folly than this
to seek the healing brush
from a garment
fringed with worldly cares

Poem 5

'My words are sandbanks'

My words are sandbanks
Your silence in spate
washes over them
Yet nothing of it
seeps down
Dommage?
I guess

Poem 6

'My word splinter'

My word-splinter
embedded
in your silence
Irritates it?

Poem 7

'Three scoops of your silence'

Three scoops of your silence
vanilla-flavoured
a sprinkling of my nutty words
dubious dessert
Care to risk it, anyone?
Not for public sampling,
says who

Poem 8

'My sequin-words'

From the soft folds
of your silence
My sequin-words peek out
spilling shiny smiles
Wish it were so!

Poem 9

'Your silence unspools'

Your silence unspools
sways in evening breeze
My words snag
on thought's barbed wires

Poem 10

'With sage steps'

With sage steps
your silence walks
sits cross-legged
under neem tree
My words play truant
from wisdom-school
run helter-skelter
kick dust and pebbles
on each path
that goes astray

At the Coffee Shop

DIVYA DUBEY

෨

'Didi, look!' Babli's excited voice broke upon Purabi's reverie. 'Isn't that the coffee shop we were looking for?'

Purabi quit her depressing train of thoughts for a moment, and pushed the red cotton skirt back to the miscellany of fashion items splayed across the desk. She looked towards the little café in the middle of the mall Babli's finger was pointing at.

Yes, there it was — *Lotsa Coffee*, the new coffee shop that had come up in place of the old Barista. It was small but swanky, Purabi had to concede, and even looked cozy without the college crowd marring the atmosphere at this hour.

College crowds had begun to get on her nerves. Was that a sign of ageing, too? The thought made goose bumps sprout on her skin.

'Didi?' Babli's voice jingled in her ear. 'That's the one, *na*, with that fat lady arguing with that man at the counter?'

Purabi joined her conspiratorial giggle and nodded. 'Shh, you shouldn't point at people like that, Babli! It's rude.'

'Oh, sorry, didi,' said Babli in English, and quickly pulled her hand back.

'It's okay,' Purabi smiled. She did like this girl a lot. If all went well, she should be able to take her under her wing soon enough — maybe as kin! The idea nestled smugly in her mind. People had begun to reproach her too much for a nonexistent personal life. Finally, she had decided to change all that. And it would be fun to mould new blood. 'You just need to learn a few things, and then you'll be a proper *memsahib.*'

'Shall we move, didi?' Babli threw her green-and-gold tassel back, pleased. 'Why, aren't you buying that red skirt?'

'No, I didn't like it.'

'Why, didi? It's so pretty. And it would suit you really well.'

'Nah, let's go.'

'But... won't you finish your cigarette first?'

The words emerged as a mumble — tentative, and uttered with a small whiff of disapproval. Purabi hid a smile. She quickly tossed the stub away, took Babli's hand, and began to walk, rapidly now, towards the new cafeteria.

By the time they reached the counter, the fat lady had left, and it was only the two of them standing on the wooden floorboards, their faces lit by soft pedestal lamps that lent an old-world feel to the place. Babli's eyes bent lily-like with deference over Purabi's Capris and stilettos as she placed the order for both of them. It made Purabi smile yet again.

'Shall we?' Purabi led the young girl away to a table for two at the corner. She carefully hung her leather bag on her chair as they sat down.

'Wow, didi,' Babli offered in English before proceeding

in Hindi. 'This shop is so beautiful! Thank you for bringing me here.'

Babli flitted and fluttered round the coffee shop, inhaling new aromas. The most commonplace things seemed to cast a spell on her, whether it was the lighting, the heavy chairs, the chequered tablecloth, or the cutlery. But then, Puabi realised, it must be all new and magnificent to her young maid. To someone who lived in a one-room hovel next to an open drain somewhere in the *jhuggi-jhopdi* colony that had illegally crept up behind the railway line, the mall and its chic shops were bound to feel divine.

'There, have it,' she said kindly, placing the cold coffee in front of Babli, whose eyes smiled like blooming Marigolds at the treat. Today, Purabi was in a mood to indulge her. She needed this distraction. She had decided to give office thoughts a holiday.

'Wow, didi, such a huge glass!'

Yes, and it probably costs one-third her salary, Purabi couldn't help thinking, as the thirsty girl washed down the contents in a single swig. Purabi, however, brooded over hers, staring and stirring at intervals.

Babli's eyes were dashing in all directions — taking in the ambience, the spectacle, the sheer variety around her. People walked in and out of the shop all the time, but her goddess-like companion barely took notice. Purabi was swimming in her own maze, her eyelids heavy, and Babli felt content just sitting where she was.

'Does this mall always remain so cool, didi?'

'I guess so. They never switch the AC off as far as I know.'

'And it's open all days of the week?'

Purabi nodded, bored.

'What fun to slip here when there's no electricity at home! You must be here quite often with your friends?'

'Friends?'

Purabi uttered the word as if pronouncing it for the first time in her life.

'Oh yes, didi!'

'I don't have any friends.'

'Oh!' Babli was stumped. 'But, how can you not? You have everything!'

Everything...

'Munna chacha told me all about your office — the polished glass doors, the giant centre table, and vases with fresh flowers.' Babli smiled, suddenly embarrassed. 'He went to drop your tiffin box one day.'

'Ah,' Purabi said drily. The servants and their extended families!

Purabi's thoughts meandered to all the people in the world who could qualify as her friends. Her unpeopled life offered her just a fistful, and Marisha was perhaps the only one who came closest.

Strange? Not really. Purabi had never had the time. She had been too busy mountain-climbing. Of a different kind. The mountain of professional excellence. Her rapid progress had put a stopcock over everything else in her life. She had joined India's largest publishing company as a junior editor, been promoted to senior editor, commissioning, and then managing editor, between a few blinks of the eye. Soon, she would be publishing manager. She could see it in that straight, dark line running deep across her palm. And she was barely forty.

Initially, Marisha had made all the effort at reconnecting. After all, they'd lived with the moniker, Siamese Twins, for a whole year at university. But the efforts were rarely acknowledged, or reciprocated, and by the time Purabi was prepared to go back, Marisha had found solace in a husband and three children instead, and had no time for any others.

There had been Harish, of course — the devoted Harish Pandit, before she turned him down and he went and got himself a wife from the States on the rebound. A fishwife, thought Purabi in disgust. Only sometimes, she missed him.

Then there was Priyamvada for a while — Priyamvada … who had tugged at her motherly emotions like none other before. She was a junior editor on her team some years ago.

Priyamvada had knelt before her like an apprentice, and Purabi, the omniscient educator, had taken her under her wing. Everybody always said Purabi had tried to run her life for her and ruined it. She insisted it wasn't true. Priyamvada had exhausted her patience, and the 'inseparable' twosome had had to be cleaved rather unceremoniously in the end.

Well, all right, she had been the one who had encouraged Priyamvada initially. She had painted a glorified picture of a career woman, imbuing her with superhuman qualities. Priyamvada had been desperate for her approval. But Purabi refused to admit that she had goaded the juvenile editor to renounce her husband and family in the process, though she had always hinted that such sacrifices were obligatory. She felt it was unfair that people should blame her for the mess Priyamvada made of her life subsequently. *She had misunderstood completely.*

After all these years, Purabi felt her brother was still perhaps the only one who did understand her. But he was well-settled with a wife and daughter in Vancouver. Purabi realised she hadn't seen him in a decade.

'…Vijay and Sheela would love this.' Purabi suddenly registered Babli's voice again.

'What?'

'If I brought my brother and sisters here, didi, they would go mad with excitement,' Babli chuckled. 'They'd love this place… and this coffee. None of us has ever had coffee before, you know. Our family believes in tea — *kadak chai.* I have to wake up at four-thirty in the morning to make it for everybody. After that, there's no water.' She wiggled her thumb. 'The taps are dry by five.'

Purabi tried to remember the last time she had woken up at four-thirty in the morning to do something. She realised she never had, except perhaps for a second round of sex with Shantanu during one of those rare, wild holidays together. Who could get up at that hour in the morning to work? And for house work of all things! That was what that woman, her mom-in-law, had expected her to do too — wake up at five every morning to take the milk. An educated elite like her, holding seminars on the Simone de Bouvoirs of the world, reduced to a prototype soap opera protagonist in her own house! Like her sister-in-law. She had tried to teach Sharmishta to stand up for herself too. She didn't believe that a wax candle like her could be galvanised into anything, least of all walking out on her asinine husband. But Sharmishta had surprised them all. Matters were bound to get complicated.

Shantanu…. Purabi winced again. She had tried to explain so much…

Her thoughts strayed away from the mall for a while. When the walls around her came into focus again a few minutes later, Babli was sitting with her empty tumbler, staring thinkingly at her.

'What happened?' Purabi found her voice again. 'Would you like another?'

Babli's face lit up. But she wasn't impolite. 'Do *you* want another cup, didi?'

'I'll have one if you will.'

'Didi!' Babli was excited again. 'Shall I place the order this time? Tell me what you want. I'll have the same.'

Purabi nodded. 'Okay, get me a latte.'

'A what?'

'Latte.' Purabi repeated slowly, and Babli pronounced it, amidst giggles, after her.

'Didi,' she said grinning again as Purabi handed her the change, 'Nobody can say I work in your house. Your *salwar-kurta* makes me look like any other girl here, doesn't it?'

Purabi studied her maid. Yes, the Rajasthani *salwar-kurta* looked good on her. For an instant she regretted having given it away. She could have worn it for a year more perhaps. But she always felt like that the moment Babli or her mother appeared in her hand-me-downs. A couple of stitches here, a corner hemmed there, a button re-stitched or replaced, a T-shirt dyed — and all her clothes were as good as new again in their hands... the clothes she so whimsically discarded at the minutest sign of defect.

Babli did look like any other girl in the mall in those clothes, slippers, and neat tresses — if a tad unsophisticated. Purabi was tempted to take her to the parlour on the second floor. Then she abandoned the idea. That would be overdoing things. Besides, she didn't have the energy. What had prompted her to bring Babli to this mall with her in the first place?

Of course, she knew the answer well. Had she not brought Babli along, she would have had to come alone. All alone. And she didn't enjoy coming here alone now. She didn't enjoy going anywhere alone any more. Sitting with her books, files, coloured pens, and laptop in her big, empty house, she had only had Babli for company for sometime now. And the girl had become more than a mere maid.

Nobody made friends in office anyway. Everybody was role-playing there. Everybody. People changed hues at will — almost like those dreadful mythical creatures. In any case, female-dominated departments like hers could barely escape the soubriquets male colleagues so callously thrust upon them — a shark pool; a snake pit... oh.

Initially, all that role-playing had been an amusing exercise: matching fake smiles with fake necklaces, and false frowns that went well with the frock for the evening.

She had enjoyed those bland kisses that vanished in the air with the perfume even before they touched a cheek, and pseudo-singsong voices venturing, '*Cottage?*' as the women's eyes scrutinised each other's earlobes.

Of late, it had become a strenuous task. The adrenalin didn't rush the way it used to once. She had surprisingly morphed into a home bird. *Shantanu would never believe it...*

Babli was there at her beck and call all evening. And that lone human voice responding cheerfully to her call every time, every day, was comforting. Sometimes she found excuses to call her, just to reassure herself. That uneducated girl from the slums meant more than the whole industry with its literati-glitterati put together now.

Purabi began digging into her doughnut. She watched Babli standing against the glass case next to the counter, looking at the jars of coffee beans with great interest.

'Coffee beans,' she explained to her when Babli returned to her seat. 'Used to make coffee.'

Babli gave her a warm smile. 'Didi, I'm certainly going to come here again. With my brothers and sisters. Certainly before my wedding.'

'Wedding?' Purabi uttered unsteadily as something went thud within. 'What wedding?'

'Oh, you couldn't have forgotten it, di. *My* wedding of course! I told you, *na*, my parents have been looking for a boy for sometime. They found one. His name's Laxman, and he works in a factory. And he goes to college, too. The wedding's in December.'

'Babli! Come on! You can't let your parents do this to you! You're barely ... what ... fifteen?'

A fizz of laughter flooded the shop. 'I'm eighteen, didi,' Babli declared with pride.

'Nah, can't be. You don't even look fifteen!'

'Well, I am,' said Babli. 'Our family's like that. A family of miniatures. Nobody looks their real age.'

Again, it was true.

When Babita had come to work for her some years ago, Purabi was shocked to hear that she was married and had six children!

'Why aren't you married, didi?' Babli asked her suddenly. 'I think you should have a very handsome husband.'

Purabi turned to her sharply, but found only an innocent question mark upon the girl's face.

'I was married,' she said quietly.

Babli looked confused. 'Married?'

'I — I divorced my husband.' Purabi felt annoyed at the effort it had taken her to utter those words in front of the little chit.

'Divorced!' Babli squealed in dismay. 'My grandmother says divorce is a very bad thing. Why did you divorce your husband, didi?'

Purabi was quiet. She sighed at the young girl's naive curiosity and imprudent questions — questions that had no prefabricated answers.

'Babli...'

'*Ji* didi.'

'Marriage is a union of two minds — remember that. It's not just about the society sanctioning sex. There must be equality in marriage — equality between man and woman. When you get married, believe in your own power. Never let the man take the upper hand; never let your in-laws rule your world; never bend your knees—'

Babli's face, tinted with silent laughter, suddenly caught her eye.

'He calls me "madam*ji*", didi,' Babli laughed. '"Madam*ji*, will you have ice-cream?", "Madam*ji*, will you come with me for a movie?" And my *saasu-ma* teases me, too. She calls me "Missej Laxman".'

Purabi stared at her servant girl — at her makeup-free face, the second-hand clothes, radiant eyes, and blissful smile. A thousand random, haphazard questions bobbed up, floated around for a while, and disappeared within her.

As she raised her eyes again, she caught her image in the mirror opposite — slender figure, a fancy black top, stone necklace, bags under pencilled eyes from too much liquor, long curls... and a single silver strand standing erect and conspicuous on her head — a brazen lock that had somehow evaded the dye this time.

'Come, Babli,' Purabi slunk herself back on the chair, and patted her young companion's hand affectionately. She reached for her handbag, rummaged around inside, pulled out her lighter, and leisurely lit another cigarette. 'Let's have another latte,' she said with a charismatic smile. 'How would you like to spend the rest of your life as a *memsahib*? Ever thought about it? Imagine... you could come here every day; be your own boss. If you are willing, I'm ready to help you.'

৪৩

Bagavathar

An Anecdote of the Seventies

SASHI KUMAR

ஜ

Bhagavathar comes riding his old, well-oiled bicycle along the quiet residential lane in Madras. Perched a notch too high on his faithful *'vahanam'*, his ear studs glinting in the morning sun, he glides down the lane unhurriedly, a stately sixty-four-year-old on his silent steed. The *angavastram*, neatly folded and compressed into a narrow strip that is the brocade margin of green and gold, is flung over the right shoulder and is in supercilious contrast to his well-worn, unpressed, aspiring white, half-sleeved cotton shirt and dhoti. Feet encased in pink-moulded plastic slippers alternate effortlessly at the pedals.

As he nears the teashop he swings his right foot, lady-like, over and across the front bar and, balancing his weight on the left foot and pedal, cruises to a halt in front of it. He props the cycle up on its stand, slides the wheel lock in and looks at his watch as he asks the shopkeeper for some betel nut. It is 6.15. There is still some time left. He reaches under his shirt and disengages his betel case from the broad multi-pocketed belt. Pulling a leaf out, he gently pats the veined side with his fingers before daubing *chunam* on it. He folds the leaf into a compact and tucks it into a corner of his mouth, following it through with the shavings of areca nut gifted by the shopkeeper.

Chewing leisurely, he lets several minutes go idly by. Then, glancing at his watch again, walks across the lane to a double-storey building. Opening the side iron gate, he pauses at the foot of the narrow open stairway that provides independent access to the two-room apartment eked out of the terrace. Ejecting the liquefied contents of his mouth in a neat red arc that hits the base of a clump of plants, he makes his way slowly up the stairs.

The old woman opens the door and lets him in.

"Haven't they woken up yet?"

"No, they were out till late last night. Shall I make some coffee?"

"No. Later. " Bhagavatar drapes the *angavastram* carefully on the hand rest of the sofa before he sits down. Where is the transistor?"

The woman looks for it in the room, but can't find it. "It must be with them," she surmises as she hurries into the bathroom to fill the buckets before the corporation supply runs out.

After restless moments spent crosschecking the time between his watch and the clock on the wall, Bhagavathar gets up and approaches the bedroom door. It is closed but not bolted from inside. He gingerly pushes the door open and enters. Mahesh and Smriti are asleep, their backs to each other. Bhagavathar moves to Mahesh's side of the bed and shakes him gently by his shoulder. "Get up. It's going to be seven."

Mahesh stirs but does not get up. Bhagavathar leaves it at that and taking the transistor radio from the bedside table returns to the other room. He leaves the door of the bedroom ajar.

The strains of Madurai Somasundaram's *Ramanaamamu* run into a medley from the bathroom — of the ascending pitch of water filling a bucket, punctuated by the swish and splash of clothes being washed. Quickly sensing the acoustic mismatch, the woman closes the bathroom door, muting the water sounds.

Ramanaamamu janmarakshakabandham... Madurai Somasundaram now has the house to himself. And a fully engrossed Bhagavathar keeping *adi tala* time with both palms and occasional appreciative grunts. "Mmmm...Aahaa..."

The new charged atmospherics evokes little response from the bedroom. Aware that time and the *keerthanam* are running out, Bhagavathar decides to step up pressure and turns   the volume up. *Somasoorya mekudaina... Ramachandunike sariyavare...* Madurai Somasundaram becomes insistent in his iterative devotion. There is a manic, tin edge to his voice pushed to levels beyond the installed capacity of a transistor radio.

Smriti is the first to respond. Her back still turned to Mahesh's, she reaches across with her left hand and jabs him in his ribs. "You better get up. Bhagavathar is waiting."

Mahesh gives in and wills his eyes open.

Kaamakotiroope Ramachandra... Kamidabalare Ramachandra...

He recognises it at once as unmistakeably Madurai Somasundaram.

But what is the raga? The question hits him like a bombshell.

Suddenly he is wide awake, his mind racing furiously to identify the raga.

It is so familiar, and so elusive.

Wasn't there a similar *keerthanam* by MS, *Nee yerangaiyenil pugazhethu…*?

In desperate hope that the raga would reveal itself to him he begins to hum softly along with Madurai Somasundaram. *Dayanaswaroopa Ramachandra… Thyagaraajitha Ramachandra…* It was a Thyagaraja *kriti* alright.

He begins to figure out the '*arohanam*'… *Sa, Ri, Ma… Sa, Ri, Ma, Pa…*

Yes, that's it! *Sa, Ri, Ma ,Pa, Ni, Sa…*

But it is tougher coming down. *Sa, Ni, Da, Pa…* And he is stuck.

Madurai Somasundaram is winding up as Mahesh emerges from the bedroom.

With an apologetic '*vanakkam*' in Bhagavathar's direction and a worried look at the clock, he makes for the bathroom in the manner of one kept from an appointment because of pressing prior work.

"What is the raga?" The challenge stops him in his tracks.

He turns around slowly and begins to hum around the contours of the raga, tentatively.

"Yes. Yes. But what *is* the raga?" Bhagavathar presses impatiently.

Mahesh gives up trying to find out and looks at Bhagavathar, importunate, expectant.

"Attaana!" announces Bhagavathar triumphantly and proceeds to delineate the raga:

Sa, Ri, Ma, Pa, Ni, Sa…

Sa, Ni, Da, Pa, Ma, Pa, Ga, Ri Sa…

As he splashes water on his face from the tap in the washbasin Mahesh curses himself for not getting it. He was almost there. It was the *Pa, Ma, Pa* bit in the '*avarohanam*' that had him foxed. Gargling noisily to make it known that he was readying his throat, he dries his face on the towel and begins to turn away from the washbasin when Bhagavatar calls out, "Please brush your teeth. We have ample time. There is no hurry."

At the teashop the quorum of morning regulars is coming alive. The samaritan, who does the honours daily, begins reading aloud from the newspaper that has just arrived, in an important, high-pitched voice. The others in the group generally lend their ears, some slurping steaming hot tea from squat hexagonal glasses. Cutting into this tea-and-news bonding comes Mahesh's higher-pitched, almost shrill 'Kalyani' from above. *Sundarinee divya...*

The reader stalls, his rhythm undone. The audience readily shifts allegiance to the singing voice scaling hazardous heights. Coaxing it on, correcting course and counselling restraint with the *gamaka*s is Bhagavathar's mellowed baritone. It is a defining moment. A few in the suborned *sada*s begin to nod and swing their heads from side to side in elaborate imitation of proper *rasika*s in proper *sabha*s.

ABOUT THE CONTRIBUTORS

ജ

Priti Aisola has written a novel, *See Paris for Me* (Penguin, 2009). She is also a poet and has written a travelogue about her journeys to different temple towns in South India. She lives in Hyderabad. Contact pritiaisola@hotmail.com

Advertising consultant by profession, **Anjana Basu** writes short stories and poems. Her novel *Curses in Ivory* (HarperCollins) was awarded the Hawthornden Fellowship in 2004. Her second and third novels are *Black Tongue* and *Chinku and the Wolfboy* (both Roli). She also works with filmmaker Rituparno Ghosh from time to time. Contact: anjanaorama@gmail.com

Kankana Basu is a Bombay-based writer whose published works of fiction include *Vinegar Sunday,* a collection of short stories, and *Cappuccino Dusk,* a novel Long Listed for the 2007 Man Asian Literary Prize. She illustrates children's fiction and assists in translating the works of her grandfather, the late Bengali author Saradindu Bandopadhyay. Contact: kankanabasu@hotmail.com

Priya Sarukkai Chabria is a poet, writer and translator. Her novels are *Generation 14* (Penguin) and *The Other Garden* (Rupa) and the poetry collections *Not Springtime Yet* (HarperCollins) and *Dialogue and Other Poems* (Sahitya Akademi). She is translating the poems of the eighth century Tamil mystic, Aandaal. She lives in Pune and is at www.priyawriting.com

Malini Chib holds two Masters degrees, one in women's studies and the other in information management. She is the Co-Chairperson of Adapt Rights Group that fights for the rights of people with disabilities, and works as Senior Events Manager, Oxford Bookshop, Bombay. Her book *One Little Finger* was recently published by Sage. Contact: mchib66@gmail.com

Gouri Dange is a Pune-based columnist and family counselor, and the author of two novels: *3 Zakia Mansion* and *The Counsel of Strangers*. Contact: gouri.dange@gmail.com

Tishani Doshi is the author of two books — *Countries of the Body*, which won the Forward Poetry Prize for Best First Collection in 2006, and more recently, *The Pleasure Seekers*, a novel, which has been translated into several languages. Since 2001 she has worked as a contemporary dancer with the Chandralekha Group in Madras. Contact: tishani@gmail.com

Divya Dubey is an author and the publisher of Gyaana Books, New Delhi. Contact: divya@gyaanabooks.com

Ramachandra Guha is a celebrated Indian historian. He was named as one of the 100 most influential intellectuals in the world. His latest book, *Makers of Modern India*, has garnered worldwide acclaim. He is based in Bangalore. Contact: ramguha@vsnl.com

Manu Joseph's first novel, *Serious Men*, is the winner of The Hindu Best Fiction Award. It is one of Huffington Post's 10 Best Books of 2010, and has been shortlisted for the Man Asian Literary Prize 2010. He is the editor of *Open* and now lives in New Delhi. Contact: josephmanu@gmail.com

Parsa Venkateshwar Rao Jr is a New Delhi-based journalist working as senior assistant editor with the *DNA*. His book, *Mullah Omar and Robespierre: The Politics of Ideas* (Rupa), a collection of his columns, was published in 2005. Contact: parsa69@hotmail.com

Meena Kandasamy is a poet, writer, activist and translator. Her work maintains a focus on caste annihilation, linguistic identity and feminism. She has published two collections of poetry, *Touch* (Frog Books, 2006) and *Ms Militancy* (Navayana, 2010). She lives in Madras. Contact: meena84@gmail.com

Acclaimed novelist, poet and critic, **Tabish Khair's** latest novel, *The Thing About Thugs*, was short-listed for the Hindu Best Fiction Prize and the Man Asian Literary Prize. He lives and works in Aarhus, Denmark. Homepage: www.tabishkhair.co.uk

Sashi Kumar is a journalist, broadcaster and filmmaker. He is Chairman, Media Development Foundation and the Asian College of Journalism (asianmedia.org), Madras. He founded the Malayalam satellite and cable channel, Asianet. His feature film, *Kaya Taran*, was showcased in festivals in India and abroad. Contact: sashi.acj@gmail.com

T Padmanabhan is an acclaimed Malayalam short story writer. His stories have been translated into almost every Indian language and into the Russian, French and the English. He received the prestigious Vayalar Award in 2001 and is also the recipient of the Vallathol Award and Lalithambika Andharganam Smaraka Puraskaram. He lives in Kannur, Kerala.

M P Narayana Pillai (1939-98) was one of the most phenomenal fiction writers from Kerala. He had worked with the Indian Central Planning Commission in New Delhi and was the Senior Assistant Editor with *Far Eastern Economic Review*, Hong Kong, before he settled down in Bombay and started writing some of the best journalistic pieces in the Malayalam ever.

Aakar Patel is a writer and journalist. He was Editor, *Mid-Day*, Bombay, before he started Hill Road Media; he writes a column for *Mint Lounge*. He lives in Bombay. Contact: aakar@hillroadmedia.com

Margaret Mascarenhas is a novelist, independent curator, consulting editor, and the Director of Goa Centre for the Arts. Author of *Skin* (Penguin India) and *The Disappearance of Irene dos Santos* (Hachette USA) she is currently working on her third novel, *Just Another Car Bomb*, and running a prison writing programme at the Aguada Central Jail, Goa. Contact: margaret.mascarenhas@gmail.com

Thachom Poyil Rajeevan is a Kerala-based bilingual writer and poet. His poems have been translated into fourteen languages including the French, Italian, Polish, Macedonian, Uzbek, Croatian and the Hebrew. He is also an acclaimed novelist in Malayalam — his novel *Paleri Manikyam* was recently adapted into an acclaimed movie, starring Mammootty. Contact: rthachompoyil@yahoo.com

Kalpish Ratna is the pseudonym under which Kalpana Swaminathan and Ishrat Syed, both award-winning and best-selling authors, write. When not reading and writing they have a joint surgical practice in Bombay. Contact: kalpana.swaminathan@gmail.com & ishrat.syed@gmail.com

K Satchidanandan is a Malayalam poet, dramatist, essayist and translator and a bilingual critic. He has over 50 original in the Malayalam and four originally written in the English, besides several edited and translated works. Winner of 24 awards (including the Kerala Sahitya Akademi Award five times) he was knighted by the Government of Italy. Contact: satchida@gmail.com

Sudeep Sen is widely recognised as a major new generation voice in world literature. His prize-winning books include *Postmarked India: New & Selected Poems*, *Distracted Geographies*, *Rain*, *Aria*, *Ladakh*, and *Blue Nude: Poems & Translations*. He is the editorial director of Aark Arts and editor of *Atlas*. A visiting scholar at Harvard University, he lives in New Delhi. Contact: sudeepsen.net@gmail.com

A J Thomas, formerly Editor, *Indian Literature* of Sahitya Akademi, New Delhi, is a poet, fiction writer, translator and literary editor. He is a winner of the Crossword Book Awards, Katha Award and the AKMG Prize. He taught English at Garyounis University, Benghazi, Libya, until he was evacuated in March 201, following the Libyan revolution. Contact: tomsaj@gmail.com

Shreekumar Varma teaches Creative English at the Chennai Mathematical Institute. He was shortlisted for the Crossword Book Award twice, and his novel *Maria's Room* was long-listed for the inaugural Man Asian Literary Prize. He was awarded the Charles Wallace fellowship in 2004. He is the great grandson of artist Raja Ravi Varma, and grandson of Sethu Lakshmi Bayi, the last ruling maharani of Travancore. Contact: varma@shreevarma.com

Farzana Versey is a Bombay-based columnist and author of *A Journey Interrupted: Being Indian in Pakistan* (Harper Collins). Her columns, feature articles and interviews on subjects ranging from politics, communalism, culture, media, philosophy and feminism have appeared in several publications over a two-decade period. She also writes poetry. Contact: farzanavee@yahoo.com

Shashi Warrier is the much-acclaimed author of *Hangman's Journal, Night of the Krait,* and *The Homecoming.* He is also an avid biker and has travelled around India on his Royal Enfield Thunderbird. He lives in Mangalore, South India. Contact: swarrier9@gmail.com

www.ingramcontent.com/pod-product-compliance
Lightning Source LLC
Chambersburg PA
CBHW051437130726
47987CB00005B/2086